OPAQUE DESIRES

BY

ANDREA AVIET

Andrea Aviet

First published in Great Britain as a softback original in 2018.

Design, typesetting and publishing by Andrea Aviet.

ISBN: 978-1-9996058-0-3

Acknowledgements

I would like to thank everyone who has helped and supported me while writing, learning how to publishing Opaque Desires.

1. Most important to God I give all the glory for giving me the strength, wisdom and knowledge to achieve all my hearts desires.

2. To my children who will learn that they inspired mum to achieve against all odds.

3. Zee Ahmed- My fantastic photographer.

4. Noveen Sheraz-Makeup artist/personal shopper. Who has worked on me for all my

promotional videos/ photo shoots. She is a close friend who is always supporting me. There is no one else I will use.
https://en-gb.facebook.com/NoveenSherazMUA/

5. Helen Bowen- who edited my book on time.

www.inthedetailcopywriting.co.uk

Introduction

Close your eyes, listen to my voice.
Feel me close, hear my heart beat,
Open your mind.
See what I see.
How does that feel?..

Join me on the journey to Opaque
Desires. Let every page of my diary
leading to sexual discovery bring you
in harmony with your inner desires.

Andrea Aviet

Lustful cravings

My body craved sex. It had been quite a while. Have you ever felt the need for that deep, longing desire? Walking down the road, carrying heavy shopping

bags, seems like a normal day after work, until; you trip over on the pavement and find yourself being picked up by a sexy, tall, broad shouldered young man. In his eyes reflect the mysteries of the world and all you desire is to uncover what lies beneath.

As he helps you up, his breath gently strokes your neck and the physical attraction is undeniable. His strong masculine arms lift you effortlessly, holding you up close and tight. The stranger glances at your lips, as if asking for your permission to lay a kiss, but instead just asks, "Are you alright?" in a husky base voice. You forget your shopping and all that captivates you is him. A feeling washes over you. You start to think you want him now, at this very moment. Every part of your physical being wants to be with him, from the sickness you feel in the pit of your stomach, to your insides turning, and yet you are aware of your surroundings and the need to keep in control. You are fighting your inner savage desires. The law of attraction is true, the sexual desires are mutual, and he asks for your name and number with a smile that blows you away. Glancing at his lips with weakened knees, lost in his eyes, you start to tell him everything. Whatever he wants is his, for the taking.

We parted ways with a thank you and goodbye.

Yet what was about to follow days later was a series of highly energetic sexual encounters and experiments. Leaving no sexual desire unfulfilled, no longing unanswered and every longing met beyond the wildest expectation.

Shall I go on? Let's share the experience together.

All I thought about was him; his broad firm chest and manly hands around my tiny waste, holding me close. He had my number. I wondered why he hadn't called...

Days passed and my desires calmed down. It was a week later, after our chance meeting, when I received a call; it was 'the stranger'.

When I first heard his voice, it took me by surprise. Instantly recognising who it was, I was excited within the first few seconds of our conversation, but that was replaced with curiosity as to why he had called?

The same husky deep voice said, "Hello. Are you there, Rose?"

"Yes."

Andrea Aviet

"How are you?"

"I am good thank you for asking, and yourself?"

"I have been thinking about our chance meeting and would like to take you to dinner, if you're free? Shall we say Friday night, 7pm?"

"That sounds perfect. Where will you be taking me?"

"It's a surprise I will take care of everything. Trust me, you're in safe hands."

"Well, okay."

"Take care Rose. I look forward to meeting you again."

"Goodnight"

Of course, there is no need to stress that I had butterflies in my stomach. Did that just happen? Did I really agree to go out on a date with a stranger, whom I knew absolutely nothing about? ...

Oh yes, I did.

There was something strange, mysterious, and captivatingly sexy about him. The way he carried his tall, elegantly masculine structure, appealed to all my senses. The feeling that had taken days to subside suddenly returned... I must have him. My entire body craved to be with him, in his arms. The urge was undeniable...

This was just the start of my Monday night and I had a while to wait... The stranger sent a message saying, "Goodnight. Sweet dreams."

Since that night, every day without fail, I received either a message or a call from the stranger, as if to keep my recently ignited interest alive. This developed into a casual bond of communication between us, whereby he tried to assure me that I was always on his mind, paving the way for what was about to take place.

Whilst the messages were casual, the calls were more hypnotic and intense in nature. The sound of his voice took the call to an entirely different level, penetrating straight into my soul, as if there was an air of enchantment encircling the conversation at both ends.

His voice had the power to command me to do his bidding, to take control of my emotions and lift me up to a level of ecstasy, all the while, just in conversation. This lead to an even greater excitement and raised the bar of expectation, paving the way for one of the most mesmerising and enchanting nights of my entire life.

He kept me so engaged that I never asked his name. Although it sounds strange, he wanted to reveal it only on our first date together, so until then, I obliged. As the day drew nearer, the excitement increased and so did questions about my likes, dislikes and was I allergic to anything?

Sweet, I thought, he is really going all out to make an effort. A man who takes note of details, cares and makes the effort is definitely worth trying out.

Imagination meets reality

Finally, it was Friday, the day I had been waiting for. My morning started with a call.

"Good morning Rose, I hope you had a good night?"

"Good morning. Yes, I did, thank you."

"That's fantastic, my beautiful lady. I look forward to finally holding your hand, and our evening together. Where can I pick you up from?"

"From outside the station, where it all began," I replied.

The stranger agreed. We were to meet that evening at 7pm. Nothing at work could alter my mental state; I was very excited and looking forward to our evening together.

In preparation for the evening I made an appointment with my beautician, for my makeup and hair to be done. The hour drew nearer and as I walked down to the station, all heads turned.

It was almost 7pm and as I neared the station, my

phone started to ring. It was him.

"Where are you my lady?"

"I'm here, at the station," I answered.

"Alright, wait there a moment. See you soon."

A tall, pleasant-looking gentleman wearing a black suit approached me, holding a mobile in his hand. He handed me the phone and said it was for me. First impressions were that this was getting far too weird for my liking. Hesitating a little, I took the phone and asked who was it? I heard the stranger's voice. It was him.

"Please let my driver bring you to me. I am waiting for you. I am sorry I could not come in person, I had to take care of some important business."

I stood there for a moment, wondering what to make of it. The driver, Adam, seemed friendly. And after all, wasn't this what I had waited for all week?

"Alright Adam; lead the way," I said, with a smile.

Adam smiled back at me and said, "This way please, follow me."

He led me to a side road where a black Mercedes was parked; he held the door open and I got in. Then he asked me if I would like something to drink, while he played some soft romantic music for me.

He poured me a glass of red wine and then sat behind the wheel.

Adam started to drive. "Where are we going?" I asked.

Looking in the mirror at me, Adam replied, "It's a surprise and I have been given strict instructions, not to breathe a word."

So, I sat listening to the music and sipping my red wine with anticipation. Within 45 minutes we were in Central London. Adam stopped the car, opened the door, and walked with me to the bank of the River Thames, where I was surprised to discover the stranger was waiting. He was standing at the foot of the gangplank of a large and beautifully kept boat. He wore a black suit, which perfectly fitted his tall, broad frame. A red tie reflected his features and contrasted prominently against his white silk shirt. He had thick black curly hair, bright green eyes, sharp features and smooth skin. His lips were a soft pink and so appealing.

As we drew near to him, Adam wished us a good evening and turned away, disappearing into the night.

The stranger took my hand in his to help me board the boat, but at that very moment, it felt like electricity flashed through my entire body, causing me to trip and him to once again have me in his arms. I was dressed in a low v-plunging front and back neckline, a short black strapped dress with nude silken stockings that poured into my black heels. My hair, in soft curls, caressed my cheeks. I seemed to be captivating the stranger's attention. He found himself lost, staring at my red lips, frozen in time.

As he held me, he whispered that I was even more beautiful than he remembered. And then, out of nowhere, he magically produced a beautiful bunch of red roses, mixed with tiny white wedding veil flowers, tied together with a red bow.

I smiled as he helped me onto the deck. I could feel his excitement, although he tried to hide it. Then he proudly gave me a tour of his boat. It was well maintained, with everything neatly kept in its place. The boat was wonderfully lit and I loved it. This was a completely new experience for me.

He took my belongings, hung my coat up and asked if my journey was alright, while looking past me, as if he was expecting someone. Then, after a few moments, he put on some music to play softly while we talked. The evening started with just the two of us. We enjoyed a beautiful conversation of discovery, our similarities, and those things that make us laugh. The attentive stranger even seemed to be a bit of a tease. His eyes glowed and his smile was distinctly mischievous.

Suddenly, he was distracted by someone calling out. He stood up, told me he would be right back, and then left me alone. He returned with a gentleman and requested that I follow him. We all stepped outside on to the deck where there was a beautiful seating area, with a white leather sofa flanked by flowers on both sides. We sat down together and the gentleman began to play a violin. I am not a great lover of the violin, but I really enjoyed the effort that had been made for me. He played the instrument beautifully. I still did not know my stranger's name. He sat close to me with his arm around my waist while I gently rested my head on his shoulder and relaxed. There was something very comforting about his presence and I found myself drawn to him, emotionally. Once the violinist finished, we applauded to show our appreciation of the music. A little later he asked, with a smile, if I was hungry and ready for dinner. Indeed, I was.

Once again, he led me to the upper decking area and there, under a starlit sky, he presented a table set for two. There were flowers all around; the white silken table cloth had a crystal vase in the centre, and in it stood a red rose. The stranger stood behind me and held my chair out for me as I sat down. I am certain he was taking note of each and every curve of my body. The dress I wore left nothing to his imagination, clinging to my body, my smooth back revealed by the plunging neckline.

Andrea Aviet

We sat down to have dinner and a waiter appeared and attended to us. It was like a dream. In the background the violinist played while whatever food we desired was served. There was a mix of Oriental dishes; just what I liked. Every detail was well thought out.

While dining, we continued to talk. The conversation flowed; it was engaging, funny and totally captivating. We held each other's interest, yet still he refused to tell me his name, maintaining the mystery.

While we sat under a blanket of stars overhead, porthole lights shone dimly along the side the boat. However, what seemed to standout even more brightly was his enthusiasm. His eyes seemed to be so focused and taking note of every detail of me. I could feel him watching me and soon I realised that the stranger didn't just ask me for dinner. We both felt the chemistry between us. He had taken care of every minute detail of the evening, trying his best to make this night perfect. He had planned it all. I remembered him asking me what kind of flowers I liked. Everything we had discussed was here. It makes you smile when a man goes the extra mile. The effort he had made to get this right was to be appreciated.

After all that's what women want, to feel beautiful, special, and to be appreciated.

For a man to care as much as we women do, was he too good to be true?!

I discovered that his family business involved a lot of travelling and he really enjoyed meeting new people, just like I do. In fact, we had quite a few common interests. In the midst of conversation, while we were still sipping our champagne and making further discoveries about each other, he stretched his hand out and said, "May I have this dance?"

Smiling and taking his hand, we stepped aside. He held me firmly yet delicately, as we danced closely; his hand on my back and my head resting on his chest. It was beautiful. Dancing with him felt magical. We stayed like that for a while with little or no conversation. We just wanted to be close, in each other's arms.

We lost track of time and soon it was early in the morning. The violinist had taken his leave and the waiter had long gone. He said he did not want me to leave and I could have my own room, if I liked. I thought it was too soon to be staying over and so despite the temptation, I decided to leave rather than stay.

The stranger respected my wishes and called for his driver. It was a truly wonderful evening and while we waited for the driver, he asked if I had enjoyed my time and if I might consider returning at a later date? But, before I could answer, he came close to me. He looked straight into my eyes and whispered that I had the most beautiful eyes he had ever seen. He thanked me for joining him and unexpectedly decided to lay a soft, gentle kiss upon my red lips.

His lips were smooth and soft and, all of a sudden, I felt a tingling in my stomach. He looked at me and smiled and I then stole another gentle kiss. There was no way I could stop him, he had me with the first kiss, which left me wanting more.

We walked slowly over to the car and he held my hand gently, as if he did not want to let go. He opened the door and I got in. "Goodbye my beautiful lady. Get some rest, we will speak soon."

In the car, I noticed a little bag which was addressed 'To Rose'. Curiosity got the better of me and on opening it, I found a chain set in silver with pink stones. It was simply beautiful. Delicate looking with Swarovski crystals and there, beside me on the other seat, was the bunch of flowers he had brought for me. How thoughtful of him. Adam asked for my address and took me home. As he drove, Adam enquired if I had a good evening and I replied, "Yes, I did, it was perfect." He smiled and played some soft music for me. In fact, it was so soothing, I fell asleep and woke up outside my home.

Within a few minutes I was indoors. All I wanted was my bed. I stripped off and got in between my soft sheets, covering my naked body gently as I lay down and fell into a deep sleep.

I had the most amazing dream; something to do with the stranger, but I could not recall exactly what it was about. I got up from my bed smiling and saw that he had sent me a message, saying he had been thinking about me. He enjoyed our first kiss and hoped it would be the first of many. My smile only grew wider and more joy-filled.

Andrea Aviet

Desires of the flesh

The rest of the day continued normally, doing exercise, having breakfast etc., but also thinking of him. What would have happened, if I had stayed?

The honest truth was that fear was the main reason that I did not stay overnight. He might have thought I was 'too easy'.

We all know when you get something easily, it is easy to lose interest, no matter how good it might be. The harder you have to work for something, the more you appreciate its value. But how hard should I make him work for us was the question, before I give in to desires of the flesh? 'What is appropriate behaviour?' is a difficult question many women have to face.

The days seemed to be long and lingering, however on Wednesday evening a call from the stranger elevated my spirits to an all new high. He asked if I was free Friday evening, as he wanted to take me out for dinner again. I said yes. How could I not, when all I wanted, all I dreamed of, was him?

That night, going through my wardrobe, picking out my dress, jewellery, shoes and handbag was on my 'to do' list. Thursday was my day to go to the beautician and so I was able to treat myself again before our meeting. I felt gorgeous and hopefully, this time, he would reveal his name to me.

Soon, it was Friday evening and the car came right to my door to pick me up. Adam knew where I lived; it was 7pm when I left to meet my stranger again. Adam asked how my week was and we made light conversation. We had formed a friendship and as Adam had known the stranger for a number of years, I knew that he was a way for me to find out more information about him. But I could wait a little longer...

"So, where are we going Adam?" I asked.

"Well, I am to drive you to Scott's restaurant where you are to have dinner, the rest is a surprise... sorry, I can't tell you anything more."

As we reached Scott's, Adam pulled up, opened the door for me and accompanied me into the restaurant until I saw the stranger walking straight towards us. He thanked Adam and, taking my hand in his, laid a gentle kiss on it while handing over a little bunch of roses. He wore a cream suit and a light brown shirt. The effect was stunning against his dark hair and light green eyes. He smiled while saying that, as usual, I looked lovely. He also complimented me on my choice of perfume.

We sat down to have dinner and talk. He said that he found me intriguing. Later we decided to go for a long walk, which is something that I really love doing; just going for a stroll on a peaceful, still night, under a star-lit sky. Life moves at such a rapid pace and so do we. Sometimes, it's just relaxing to walk and listen to nothing but stillness.

After the walk, we decided to go for a drive. Adam drove while we just sat in the plush back seat, relaxing in each other's arms. Then he suddenly said, "Stay with me", and gently laid a tender kiss upon my lips.

Driven by emotion and impulse, and rejecting my better judgement, I said, "Yes." He smiled and asked Adam to return to the boat while he kept his arms wrapped around me, as if to say, you are safe and you belong to me now.

We got to the boat and it was nearing 1.30am. Inside the cabin, I felt it was going to be a long night. The stranger played some music softly in the background. It was love songs and he poured two glasses of wine. Then he made a toast, "To strange coincidence and chance meetings." While adding that he found me to be a rare beauty. Most flattering words.

Taking my hand in his he said, "May I have this dance?" I obliged and he held me close, so close that once again I could feel his breath upon my cheek and his heartbeat against my cheek. He looked at me strangely, as if he was trying his best to read my thoughts. While he did so, he bent down and I felt his lips upon mine once again. With one hand around my waist and the other at the side of my face, the kiss became more passionate and soon our tongues found each other.

His hands slid up the sides of my waist, further up, until his hands gently caressed the sides of my breasts, brushing past them, sending electric shocks and shivers through my body. He became more passionate and while he was gentle and took control, he was not overpowering, rather moving in consideration of my feelings. I was backed up against a wall. He stood in front of me with one leg in-between mine, giving me the impression that he wanted to tear my clothes off at that very moment and have wild passionate sex with me. He pressed up against me while one of his hands gently slid up my thigh. He wanted me to crave his touch and all I wanted at that moment was to feel him inside of me. He began to kiss my neck, my collar bone and buried his face in my tender breasts. He glanced up into my face and saw my expression of complete surrender. He took me by the hand and, stroking me tenderly, he led me downstairs. The lights had been dimmed. In the centre of the room was a bed with white silk sheets, red rose petals scattered all over on it. In the centre between two pillows lay a single red rose. On the left wall was a television. The other side had a huge mirror and small seating area. It was a lovely bedroom. The headboard was ornate and made of cast iron. As he walked, he smiled and asked if I liked the room.

"Yes", I replied, "it's beautiful."

He had created an impression which we would both remember. He started kissing me passionately, while slowly undoing my zip. His hands slid right down my back, onto my bear flesh. Feeling the softness of my back, feeling every curve and down my spine. He commented that mine was one of the sexiest backs he had ever felt. Then he slid my dress straps off, first one side over my shoulder and then the other. My dress fell to the floor.

He smiled, as if he was capturing the moment and treasuring the mental picture of what he had just uncovered. Sitting at the edge of the bed, his coat was long-gone. I sat across his lap, sliding one leg across and passionately kissing him in return. Simultaneously, I slowly unbuttoned his shirt, undoing one button at a time. I discovered a smooth muscular body with a few tattoos. It was so perfectly defined and looked like a sculpted model. My hands just did not want to stop exploring.

The smoothness of his skin, his intoxicating aftershave, the dim lights and being so close to him, just unleashed my wild, passionate side. There was no holding me back now. His scent sparked off a chain-reaction, embedding my teeth into the side of his neck and softly biting him. The wildling in me had been unleashed. Still feeling his every muscle and reaching down to loosen his belt while our passionate kiss continued. Suddenly, he stood up, with my legs wrapped around his waist and my arms around his neck. As I held on to him, he held me up, supporting me firmly with both hands under my buttocks. He could feel my black satin underwear and the well moistened skin on my smooth legs. He turned to the side of the bed and knelt on it while lowering me gently. Placing me on top of the rose petals and handing me the single rose. He could have me all night on that bed, just kissing him and laying close by his side, hearing nothing but the sound of his heartbeat.

He ran his hands all over my body, exploring every curve. It felt like nothing I have ever felt before. He made me laugh, he was so caring. He asked if I was okay. I found it sweet that he thought to seek permission before continuing... like a true gentleman.

Of course, I gave my consent. He came closer and looked into my eyes as he gently slid his hand up my soft thigh. He remarked on how much he liked a curvaceous lady, who had taken care of her figure. After that there was no part of my craving body that his lips did not explore. From my neck, to gently rubbing my breast, from sliding the thin straps of my lingerie off my shoulders, to sucking on my breasts, causing me to sigh with pleasure. Turning my nipples harder and sending goose bumps throughout my body. His tongue went around and around my nipples, and he started sucking on them gently, then harder, and a mixture of feelings ran through me. The pain of the biting turned into pleasure, causing me to let out a little scream, experiencing inexplicable thrills. I dug my nails into him, leaving long scratch marks down his back. He held my hands gently above my head with one hand, and whilst I wanted him to stop, my body craved for more. It was a losing battle, one that the flesh would win. He was the flautist and I was the flute. He played me with perfection. His hands ran down my flat stomach, followed by his tongue. When he slid my underwear off, I was completely in his hands, at his mercy, a slave to his will, as I lay there on his bed.

The stranger had his way with me. He massaged my body with oil to help relax my muscles, tense from daily life. It felt like my body was a blank canvas, ready for him to make his mark. He said, "I want you to be comfortable and I don't want to rush you into anything you're not ready for."

When he saw my body covered in goose bumps, he drew a beautiful embossed white sheet over me and then lay close, with his arms wrapped around me. So strange was the feeling inside, the craving subsided a bit, as we lay together, flesh upon flesh and nothing in between. Legs wrapped together. I felt a closeness, and a calmness, a sense of satisfaction and contentment. A sense of bonding and belonging.

We talked as we lay in bed and an hour or so later he remarked "You're so beautiful... I am sorry, but I am finding it really hard to stay away." As he uttered the words he initiated a kiss, which reignited the passion of the night. He pulled himself across the bed and on to my chest. I could feel his masculine muscles. His strong hands took a firm hold of my buttocks and squeezed them, running his tongue down between my breasts. He parted my thighs to get his head between them and buried himself into position. Going down on all fours, his tongue penetrated deep inside my vagina, while he sucked, licked and flicked my clitoris and inserted his tongue in and out in a motion of perfection. I moaned with ecstasy. The pleasure was overwhelming, I couldn't handle any more of his long, soft, tongue. It was too much, he was too good and it felt as if my insides were about to explode. He kept me deep rooted by holding onto me firmly and said, "Relax and enjoy the moment." The sheets were being pulled in all directions as I let out moans of pleasure.

Andrea Aviet

Erotic play

When he stopped so that I could catch my breath, I noticed that he was rock hard, a perfect moment to penetrate, since after his tongue stimulation I was very moist and ready for it. He looked into my eyes and, without a word, kissed me again passionately as he penetrated. He went in deeper and deeper, holding me down, raising one leg and then manoeuvring, adjusting himself to be completely within the tight, warm, wet walls of my vagina. And when he found that comfortable place, he smiled and asked again if I was okay. I was speechless, but collected myself together to get a response out, and said, "Yes."

I could feel him moving inside of me as he started again, slowly pushing himself in and out. He wanted to climb inside me. Then the stranger said, "look into the mirror for me." I have to admit that watching yourself having sex in a mirror is very erotic.

As I turned to look into the mirror, he pushed in deeper and deeper which made me moan, and then he whispered in my ear, "my name is Edward." I could hardly believe my ears. When he stopped, and after catching my breath, I enquired if I had heard him correctly? I called out, "Edward?"

"Yes", he replied, and continued pleasuring me again until we were both tired and in need of rest.

Edward was such a lovely name. He was so sexy and left my every desire fulfilled. He wanted our night to be one that we would both remember, and that's why he felt it was so important that I looked into the mirror to see him thrusting, whilst hearing his name. I will remember that image, always.

It was a night I would never forget. As I gasped for breath, with sweat pouring down my back, I knew that I would never forget Edward. Sex is not just about two people becoming intimate and giving into sexual desire. It's not about rushing the entire moment in the height of passion. It's about taking your time, giving pleasure, and enjoying the foreplay, which leads to the build-up. It's a skilful art, which needs careful thought, strategy, the perfect environment and setting. Along with perfecting the skill of exploring each other's body and building up to that final moment of ecstasy, climax and release. The art of achieving an organism and reaching that point of satisfaction and fulfilment, is taking care in perfecting your skill and paying attention to each other's physical, emotional and psychological desires.

Edward was a perfectionist; he knew what he was doing and aimed to satisfy and please his partner in bed... When I say satisfy, there was no position we did not try. It was so energetic, experimental and exciting. Edward concentrated on the smallest details. Massaging my body and gently running his fingers all over me. Then repeating it harder, putting more energy and force into the same action.

We lay down together on the bed. I felt safe in his arms, under the sheet. He kissed me goodnight and said I was perfect; he enjoyed every part of me. He enjoyed us. Edward was a phenomenal kisser; he was gifted in the art of kissing and gave it an entirely new meaning. I fell off to sleep, smiling.

Waking up in the morning, I found Edward lying still by my side and saw that he was observing me. He had a smile on his face and as I looked up into his face, he laid a gentle kiss upon my lips.

"You sleep so peacefully", he remarked and asked if I was hungry.

"Yes, thank you", I replied.

Edward got up to fetch a robe for me and as he got out from under the covers, he left me staring at his well-defined body. The morning's natural light showed it off even more than I remembered. The darkness of the night did not do justice to his physique. Edward teasingly asked, "You like what you see?" and came towards me sliding back in under the sheets, after dropping the robe down on the bed. He put his arms around me once again and laid by my side. Last night's excitement returned. It was new, exhilarating and a wonderful experience and before we knew it, we were enjoying each other again. Early in the morning is one of the best times to have sex. The light makes a difference with its natural energy. It just gives you a very different feeling. We decided to shower together and then dress for breakfast. It was a perfect night and an equally perfect morning. During breakfast he asked if there was anything more he could do for me before I left. Edward said he did not want me to leave, but knew I had other commitments and so looked forward to our next meeting.

Edward was the perfect gentleman. Polite, well mannered, handsome, a good kisser, generous, romantic and caring. He stood up each time I did. He helped me out of my chair and as we finished breakfast, he had a small parting gift ready. He said I could open it if I wished. Needing no more encouragement to open the little square box, I did. Inside it lay a silver chain with a little heart pendant and a small white diamond stone on one corner. It had a set of matching earrings and it was the most beautiful, thoughtful present anyone had ever given me. "I love it, thank you Edward" and I gave him a kiss and a hug. He was happy, pleased to find that I appreciated his little gesture and walked me to the car, wishing me a safe journey back home.

Andrea Aviet

In the car Adam remarked that I looked very happy.

"It's a rare surprise to find a man like Edward who ticked all the boxes," I replied. Adam smiled and nodded.

Reality of life

Within me, I felt a sense of joy, fulfilment and hoped that this would turn into something special. My outlook in life is that, unless you try you never know. I believe everything in life is a chance, a coincidence. Even relationships are like taking a chance, something like a lottery system. So I was willing to try and give us, me and Edward, a chance to work

After reaching home and trying to catch up with all the necessary daily activities, I addressed the mixture of feelings I held within. I was trying to concentrate on daily chaos yet getting distracted by thoughts of Edward. I badly wanted to pick up the phone and hear his voice, although we had parted ways only a few hours ago.

I was behaving like a young naive girl.

I had no doubt that Edward, however, was busy getting on with his business meetings and planning the future of his company. Our time spent together for that moment had come to an end, and now, I'm sure it was back to work and the next important agenda for him.

The day passed by quite well. Anyone who has had any kind of sexual encounter that leave them fully satisfied, knows exactly the impact on mind, body and soul. If you have had a really good experience of sex, it's refreshing, energising and makes you more creative. Yet if it's not a good experience it just leaves you annoyed, wanting more, leaving you feeling irritated, unfulfilled.

Although his thoughts lurked in my mind, I gave Edward the space he needed. Late that very same night, Edward sent me a text saying he hoped I'd had a good day and that he was thinking of me but was extremely busy with work. He wanted to wish me a good night and sweet dreams. He ended his message with a few kisses.

Receiving a message from him just lit up my face. I sent him a coy, yet flirtatious response.. Throughout the week the same routine continued. Edward would text and call. Sometimes he just turned up in the evening, unannounced, and ask me to get ready for dinner. I knew he was a lot busier than I was so whenever he made the effort to make time for us I obliged in return. Some days we would go out for a meal and a long walk just spending time together. I missed him badly when he went off on his business trips. When he returned he would spoil me and we would end up becoming passionately intimate. Each time got more erotic, more experimental and absolutely unforgettable.

Edward was a mature, intelligent, business man while I was a young, irresponsible girl, caught up with infatuation. I confused what existed between us with love. Yes, the mistakes many young ladies make.

One day, as I lay in bed waiting for Edward to return, his phone rang. I thought nothing of it and answered the call. I had come to think of myself as his girlfriend because we slept together and he made me feel so special. Of course, answering his phone would not be an issue. A lady on the other end asked who I was.

"I am Rose. How can I help you?" I replied

Her voice sounded shocked. She started to cry and disconnected immediately. When Edward returned I told him about the phone call. I related the entire incident to him. Edward checked the number and told me not worry about her, it was nothing. But it bothered me and I wanted to know why she was upset. Call it a woman's intuition, but I knew there was something amiss. I felt very uneasy. Aalthough Edward said to let it go, I really and truly could not.

Days passed. Edward was fantastic. He continued to spoil me, treat me like a treasured possession. But I could be entirely happy like before, because the thought of that phone call had upset me. I wondered about that day. Until that point there was no need for me to be suspicious of him. I had been able to just enjoy his company and hope that one day we would learn to be together and commit to each other.

Edward had another business meeting coming up, so he had to go away for a few days. He asked if I would be here waiting for him on his return. I told him yes, but an uneasiness made me unsure whether I actually meant it.

While Edward was away this time, he called fewer times. The messages were fewer too and my heart sank. I knew something was not right. Edward returned a few days later. He hadn't told me when to expect him, but I found out because Adam arrived with a huge bouquet of red roses. The note attached, read: "I missed you, when can I see you? xx"

It was sweet. It made me smile. Edward cared; he missed me.

A little later, a mental argument took place in my head. Two thought patterns ran parallel; one yes, I'll go and see him, the other no, if he was too busy to text perhaps I am not important enough for him to miss in the first place? I struggled back and forth. But I was young and foolish, so I asked Adam to wait for me, while I got changed.

Player's paradise

Edward was surprised. As I entered he embraced me tenderly and we kissed. Perhaps he had missed me?

Then he sat me down and my heart stumbled. Edward said he wanted to talk to me about something. He told me he loved his life, he loved beauty but it was also his weakness.

"I can feel the change in you since you heard that lady's voice on the phone, last time we were together," he confessed, gently stroking my hand. "She was one of the ladies I met prior to finding you. I have wined, dined and showered affection on many women before." His eyes fell as he explained this to me. He let go of my hand.

He went on to tell me that it was over between them but she could not let go. She missed him and loved him. My eyes opened wide and although I didn't want to hear the answer I knew the question had to be asked. So, I mustered the courage and asked Edward, "What do you feel for me? What is this we share, how would you categorise it?"

Edward took my hands in his and looked deep into my eyes. "I enjoy spending time with you. I enjoy us having sex, but I can't commit to a relationship." As he said this he kissed me. In return all I felt was hurt. My eyes filled with tears. What we had was fairly new but I had secretly hoped we could move towards a relationship. If it didn't work out, a breakup. But to know that Edward just did not want to commit from the outset, well it just wasn't what I was looking for.

"You're upset," he whispered. "I am sorry, I never wanted to hurt you."

I allowed myself to be swept away by him one last time, but then I asked Edward never to contact me again. I ended us.

I left straight away, not wanting to wait around to see if time might change his mind. He was too preoccupied; the risk of investing my feelings in hollow hope was too big.

He had too many women; it's not that it was too much competition for me. I wanted no competition, a real relationship like any other woman would expect. Months passed by. I needed time to heal and move on. I understood why the other lady had been hurt. Edward had gained my trust and confidence by treating me exceptionally well. Exactly how a man should treat a woman. He raised the bar so high for all other men to follow in his footsteps. An impossible task.

Even after a few months, Edward still crept into my thoughts. Why did he never try to contact me? Did he miss me? Random thoughts would go through my head, but all I wanted was to stop missing him and put him from my mind.

Andrea Aviet

1st January -Pornography, obsession

My heart longed for Edward. I knew I wasn't giving myself enough recovery time and I rushed into the next relationship that came along. I needed a diversion from Edward so anyone's open arms would have done. Along came Jim.

This man was complicated; his family life growing up was disturbed and he had many failed relationships. But I was hurting and clarity of thought was not something I had at that moment. The sex wasn't good. In fact, it was a major let down. I think the main cause was that he was addicted to porn and role play. But he wasn't even a good role player.

Jim failed to distinguish between fiction and reality. He thrived on the fake, the over exaggerated, the extreme facial expressions and screams of pleasure right down to the loud sighs. To get into the mood, he had to watch porn first. He had grown so used to 'doing himself' that the need to actually have sex was almost non-existent. Either he was tired or not in the mood. Even dressing up to get him interested did not help.

I was young and still held the memory of Edward. Which made me crave sex badly. But here was Jim, who could not (or would not) perform. In casual conversation I remember asking Jim why he never went down on me. His reply was that he was no good at it. His other girlfriends had said so. He was reluctant to do it.

Being physically unsatisfied left me wanting and I was annoyed at the total uselessness of Jim. He was no good. he fantasised about his lady dressing up as an air hostess and having sex in public. Seeing too many movies had actually spoilt his chances of having a normal, healthy, working relationship, especially since no amount of dressing up would actually excite him. No other partner other than his very own hand could give him the exact pleasure he craved. He was so addicted to fantasy that he couldn't handle true intimacy, reality; I knew I had to end it right away.

Jim failed to recognise that entering into a relationship meant you needed to try and make the effort to be there for each other in every way. The easiest way should have been the sexual interaction, even if it was role play. Yet for all that, it seemed to be the worst part of our relationship. If a woman is not satisfied, it leaves her looking for someone who can fill the void.

Unsurprisingly, my relationship with Jim failed, it was a mess; the new man was no comparison to Edward. Yes, we slept together but all it did was make me yearn for Edward. As quickly as it began, it ended. Regret took hold of me. All he liked was gambling, drinking and porn. Clubbing, drinking and dancing all seemed a good distraction at the time. But nothing could erase the loss or pain I felt inside. I was looking for healing in the wrong places and it had led to even greater misery and a void which nothing could fill.

15th January – Life is not a bed of roses

Something had to change. So, I stayed away from the dating scene.

That's when I realised that the old adage 'Time is the greatest healer' was too true. Perhaps time was what I needed?

I received a call from an old friend, Jillian, early one morning. She was more of an old acquaintance really, but she needed my help. She'd had a really wild night out and had ended up drinking and having group sex. She'd drunk too much and had woken up with a hangover, in a strange place. She needed my help to get home.

Jillian was 21 and very experimental in nature. She said she just needed to get fucked, but had ended up having a threesome and a lot to drink. When I picked her up she told me all about her evening; that she was fully satisfied and had an amazing night but was a little sore, especially since she consented to anal style too. But she'd enjoyed it thoroughly. I managed to get Jillian home without her throwing up, a fact I was quite proud of.

She somehow reminded me of myself, lost and making silly mistakes. This was a lifestyle that I was neither happy with, nor proud of. Unlike her though, I was not a young girl. I was supposed to be a young lady. There is a fine line between a girl and a lady. A girl is young, a girl is naïve. A lady should be mature, elegant and dignified. Still, I lacked these qualities. The girl in me was going through challenges and had not crossed over completely into becoming a lady. Seeing my young friend in this condition made me look at myself. It was like realisation striking. I began to question myself: do you want a life like Jillian? I still struggled to find my way and discover love. It was not easy. I battled my innerself, I battled my emotions, my surroundings. But it was all for a good reason. Eventually the struggle led to me submerging myself in work.

It certainly kept me occupied and gave me the added advantage of building up my finances. Yet everyday, once I returned home, so did the memories of Edward. But working so hard did not leave much room for thinking. Tiredness got the better of me most nights and as soon as my head touched the pillow, my eyes would just shut. The same routine continued for days.

Life became monotonous and soon, feelings of longing for someone, anyone, started to resurface. Being young, beautiful and single did not fit well for me.

In the days to come I started to realise that most of the people around me were not very happy. Something was missing from their live;, quite a few had money problems, bills to pay and were barely making ends meet, others had different issues. Marital complication, partners not being faithful, disagreements, fights. The list was endless.

I couldn't find one couple in my circle that was truly satisfied, content and happy to be with each other. And yet, in pursuit of happiness, I thought that being in a relationship, having someone with me to share my evenings and weekends, would bring me happiness. I loved the idea of having a partner, cooking together, sharing dinner, being looked after and having someone to look after, would be nice. Well that's the mind of a woman.

For men it's entirely different. They usually don't think about relationships, bonds and togetherness. It's more about career, seeing to one's own self-interest, meeting friends, going to the gym. And if they feel like having sex, going to a bar, meeting someone and then spending the night together, is usually no big deal. It's all in the heat of the moment and needs must be met.

Harry was a prime example. He was stopped at a red light when he saw this babe. She had huge tits, a big ass, she was curvy and well-built. He came in to work with an erection, saying he wanted ask her to hop in his car and take her, there and then. This had brought back memories for him, flash backs to when he was younger, on holiday in Spain, and he'd

Andrea Aviet

befriended a babe. She had long blonde hair, right down to her waist and the sexiest figure he had ever seen. Harry explained that they went for a drink and she ended up sliding her hand up his trousers, rubbing him, venturing to undo his zip and then started sucking him off while he was driving her home. It got that far that he had to pull up, parking the car in a safe spot. That's when she slid across and rode him till he ejaculated while he sucked on her breast. He remembered how good she was and how well she rode him. Harry, in the middle of the office, had become hard again, thinking about his holiday tryst. We asked him to leave, take a trip to the toilets and only come out when he was more self-composed.

While some women can behave like that, we general form some sort of attachment, even if they don't want to unlike men.

18th January – Rushed love

And so, back to me. I kind of got evolved with yet another man. He was caring towards me, I knew he was genuinely in love with me and would do anything I asked. I was still upset with my own circumstances, but not once did I take advantage of him.

Unfortunately, he was a married man; he managed to capture my heart with his kindness. The mental bond grew between us and I saw how much he cared. Everyone who saw him by my side knew he had feelings for me. So, nobody believed that we could be so close without crossing any limits or boundaries.

Why do people rush into things?

Richard had fallen in love with me, everyone could see it. His wife had been unfaithful and he found it hard to forgive her. To be unfaithful is one thing, but to sleep with Richard's sister's husband? Yes, his wife and brother-in-law. He was devastated. But he didn't want to destroy his own sister's marriage, so he kept it quiet, holding on to this shocking secret. He would avoid family gatherings at all costs. His mum couldn't understand her son's estranged behaviour and became upset. This put a lot of stress on the entire family. His wife's unfaithfulness and betrayal had caused a rift in his family and called his loyalty in to question. It was painful to keep this secret sealed within him. But one day he opened up and told me everything.

Richard loved his children more dearly than anything else in this world; that's what made him a fantastic father – another quality of his which I admired. I had never wanted to be the cause of anyone's marriage breaking down, which is the main reason I had for keeping my distance physically. Had I been so inclined, there were plenty of opportunities for us to sleep together, plenty of hotels all around in the area... But that just wasn't me. Let me make myself clear. If a marriage is standing on the rocks, so be it. But I never wanted to be the cause of the break down. Nor did I want Richard to leave his wife for me. I stressed to Richard that, if he left his wife, he was doing so because he did not want to be with her anymore, irrespective of whether I came to him or not. The best part about this entire ordeal was that I felt I managed to heal the relationship between a mother and her son.

One day I asked Richard whether he loved me.

"You know I do" he assured me.

Women like to put men to the test and we are rather good at it. Most of us can recognise whether a man is really in love, or just faking it. But in some cases, we only see what we want to see, hear what we want to hear. Richard's reaction to his mother had surprised me. I wanted him to call her and explain why he stayed away. Tell her the reason he never attended family gatherings. Perhaps by forgetting the bitterness and letting the truth, no matter how hurtful, be revealed, everyone would be set free.

Richard agreed to try. He called his mother to explain. At first, she was very surprised. Later, her surprise turned to shock. Not only did he tell her about his wife and her affair with his brother-in-law, but he also went on to inform his mother that he was in love with me. Wow, that left us both speechless for a while...

She asked him to think about his children, not to make any rash decisions. Just like any good mother would do, she advised her son the best way she could, not wanting his family to breakdown, or for the children to be abandoned or hurt.

We all want a man who will truly love us for who we are, but at what cost? I couldn't take a loving father from his children or break up a family. That had never been my intension. Richard tried hard to convince me of his love, but he knew where we stood.

"Why did you marry your wife? Were you in love with her?" I asked him over dinner one night. His answer surprised me. They had been family friends. Close, but not in love. He thought he would never find anyone, so when she proposed he just went along with the situation and agreed to marry her.

"Wow" I gasped. "You settled for her? You weren't in love?"

"Yes, I'm afraid I did. Now I realise it was the worst decision I could make." He looked devastated.

We remained friends. I couldn't take our relationship any further but he would always have a special place in my heart because there was a genuine connection between us. To the outside world, no boundaries were ever crossed. You don't plan who to fall in love with and if we could have chosen, we wouldn't have feelings for each other. But it's my firm belief that, no matter what you feel, you can always stay in control of your actions and how far you take a relationship. I remained in control.

On one occasion, Richard told me that he wanted out of his marriage. He reassured me that I was not the cause; her unfaithfulness had hurt him so deeply that he could not stay in the relationship with her anymore. He did not want to return home, he wanted space to think. It was the right thing for me to do, to try and help him. I tried to find a friend to put him up overnight, but no one was able to help. I booked him into a hotel instead. Richard was grateful, because he needed time to think, space away from his wife and family. Hurt was destroying him; he loved his kids but was not in love with their mother. I took him to the hotel. It was a bitter, wet day. I dropped him right outside the hotel door and turned to leave. Richard asked me to stay.

That was the hardest decision to make. There was nothing holding me back. Who would know if I stayed? There was no one there, nothing stopping us from going ahead. And we both felt strongly for each other...

But I couldn't. I had to think of Richard, of his children, and of his wife – the lady who did not know I existed. I knew, if we crossed that line he would have been mine forever. He wanted a definite level of commitment from me that I would be his. I know that sometimes, people don't like to be alon. But at the same time, I knew it would tear him apart. He loved his kids, but if we slept together before he'd made the final decision to leave, it could damage his relationship with them. Richard would be no better than his wife. So, for the love of him, I turned away.

"I'm sorry."

I hoped, eventually, he would understand the sacrifice I made; I really wanted to stay. I was in need and extremely vulnerable. But, I am found some strength. Maybe it came from above? That's the best way I can describe it. Sometimes you connect with one special person from deep within your soul, and that connection remains, no matter what happens. But for all that, all I could offer to Richard at that time, was friendship.

Perhaps life would have been different if only he hadn't rushed to commit simply because he was afraid to be alone? If he had considered the possibilities of what could be? Many of us rush: we rush life, we rush decisions, we rush everything, because we are afraid to lose what we right then. In case nothing better comes along. We are afraid of missing out.

Fear is the key ingredient for trouble.

If only he'd had the confidence in himself, to know that no matter what, he would survive. Who knows what might have become of us? I had to put him down; it was not meant to be. It's better to let someone go and set them on their own path, especially if they have, as Richard had, already committed to being with someone else.

There was nothing I could do to stop Richard from loving me. But at least this way, his family stayed together, loveless marriage or not. I know I still hold the key to his heart, although that is one door which, from my side, will always remain closed.

After Edward and then Richard, life got extremely tiring. Edward, the perfect romantic, had been an infatuation. Richard was real. He was down to earth and we formed a special connection deep within ourselves. But, heartbreakingly, I had to draw on my inner strength to do the right thing and walk away.

Andrea Aviet

3rd February –Good girl, gone wrong

The days following my decision to walk away from Richard were very dark. I began to question my decisions, which led to a series of follies and bad judgements. I was tired of being a 'good girl'.

I wanted to lead a life of excitement, experience adventure and just live for the moment, not worrying about telling about right from wrong. All that mattered to me now was being happy and living each day thinking of myself, alone. It sounded wonderful I theory, but in practise it was a messed-up time for me. I was selfish and ended up getting annoyed and hating myself. It had begun to be aggravating to be my old self – caring, thoughtful and selfless. So, I strove to be free from myself. My friends thought I was a mess, ignorant, foolish, and a screw up. None of them understood that all I required was guidance and understanding. I was still innocent and quite gullible. But I thought being open and talkative, viewing others in my likeliness, would help me move on from my old self. This was the worst mistake I could have made, though, as people were cruel with their mockery and scorn, hypocritical female friends turned to slanderers and I became the subject of everyone's chatter. The gossipers gossiped, the slanderers slandered yet I continued on the same path, not knowing how to change.

When hurt rules and loneliness becomes your closest friend, it's easy to fall into anyone's arms. I needed to fill the void inside me so I looked for happiness in the arms of men, hoping to find my soulmate, someone who would make me whole again. My continuous journey, searching for true happiness and inner peace. The days passed by and I began to wonder, with heartfelt regret, how I had ever started down such a road. But down the road of follies I continued, unable to come up with a way to turn my life around.

Finally, a co-worker suggested trying online dating. Oh, that was new, adventurous. It sounded exciting to be presented with so many choices without the pressure of meeting anyone until I was really sure about them. I could make my decisions based on ,mutual interests, likes, hobbies... I realised I knew so many couples who had found each other through dating sites, so my interest was piqued. With such evidence to hand, it seemed to be a fantastic idea.

Sam, a friend of mine who never held back, had earned himself the title of 'play boy'. His solution to every problem in life was good sex, women, drugs and more sex. Online dating was his suggestion for a gentler approach to meeting new people. His approach was worlds apart. Every time he spotted a woman who appealed to him, he had her number within five minutes – such confidence. I don't know how he managed it, but he was a smooth talker. He talked constantly about his manhood. He always bragged openly that he could satisfy any woman and have her screaming his name out loud. He could go a long while without stopping and had a good length and thickness to 'Sam junior' – his nick name for his so called best asset. So does size matter? Well it depends rather on the individual and his performance skills. Sam delighted in explaining that, there was a fine line between hitting that 'special place' and delivering delicious orgasms and being capable of longevity but not really being any good at it...

Well, size matters for some men and not for others; the same goes for women. I've heard some women say that they can't handle men who have a larger penis as it's too painful; instead of pleasure, all they feel is pain. While others say the bigger a man's penis, the better the penetration and therefore the more the satisfaction.

On the flip side, some men like petite females, while others prefer bigger, curvier women. There's a lot to be said for 'something to hold on to', while others prefer their women to fit snugly into their arms with no extra padding. Some women like well-built men, whereas others like slim-built. The result of our discussion? Variety and diversity is the spice of life. But one thing is clear: the right proportion and mix of stamina and skill could elevate anyone to ecstasy.

Back to online dating. The idea of setting up an account was just purely for fun. No expectations other than to kill time and banish loneliness. It was rather exciting and fun. Men approached me with flattering words, trying to get me to respond. I dissolved into laughter many times while reading their various attempts at seduction. It kept me occupied from within the privacy of my own home, without having to go anywhere to meet people.

That's when someone got my attention. A gentleman reached out, telling me that my profile picture was one of the most beautiful pictures he had seen. His looks were simple, nothing outstanding. In fact I ignored the message for a few days, only returning later in a bored moment. I decided to respond because his message was kind, nothing over the top.

He replied to my message and we chatted for a while. It was new so of course it was exciting. We exchanged numbers and finally, one day, he asked permission to call. We chatted for hours. And then we continued our conversation on text and WhatsApp. He was very attentive. He said he wanted to know what I was doing every minute of the day. He seemed quite decent and genuine at the time. We exchanged some life stories and we finally agreed to meet.

Andrea Aviet

During our first meeting, I have to admit, I wasn'y too impressed with the way he looked; his physique needed some getting used to. I like well-built men. He was quite the opposite, so it put me off from the very start. I just wanted to go home, so the conversation didn't exactly flow. As the evening progressed he tried his very best to maintain my attention and as the days passed and we continued to chat, his efforts did pay off. I got used to the calls, the texts, meeting up and just spending time together, until one day he asked me over to his house. I was quite shocked that he lived in a house share with two other women. Perhaps I'm a little old fashioned, but I found that strange. Later, I discovered they were friends his ex-girlfriend. After they split, he needed a place to live. He'd moved in with them. Friends advised me not to be negative or narrow minded, but rather to be open to the fact that he was a young working professional and needed to be cut the costs of bills. Even though I could not quite put my finger on it right from the word go, something just did not add up. My intuition was advising me against taking my relationship with him any further.

When he asked me over saying to his place, I sought the advice of my friends. He'd told me that no one else had been to his place before. My friends pointed out that, if he were a player, he wouldn't want me at his house, especially if he was messing around with house mates. Perhaps I should give him the benefit of doubt? I decided to keep my mind open. But this proved to be a real challenge.

Mark seemed alright. He was caring and attentive, but something just didn't feel right. He carried baggage from his past; he said he had broken up with his ex-girlfriend and had moved on. He longed for a new relationship, for commitment and we talked about that at length. I wasn't sure whether Mark was trying to prove his long-term commitment to me, or whether he was just telling me what he thought I wanted to hear. But I did notice that one of his housemates seemed rather interested in him. There had just been some comments from her, added to the fact that she couldn't look me in the eye whenever we met. Yet, when Mark spoke she would come alive, be very cheerful and interactive, focusing only on him. He would often tell me that she asked a lot of questions about us, what we were doing and where we were going.

A few incidents stood out to me; a woman's intuition should never be ignored. I like to look good and going to my beautician was one of the things I would do regularly. I changed my hair colour one day and Mark's housemate went to get hers done too. She said it had taken five hours.

"I can't believe it took five hours! I've never sat in a chair for so long."

For all that, she was rather excited that Mark liked the way her hair looked.

The next incident I remember is that we had planned a night out. We were supposed to be going clubbing but when I arrived to see Mark, plans had changed. Mark had been out the night before, with his housemate and a group of her friends. They'd stayed out until the early hours and Mark had had no sleep. He didn't want to go clubbing with me, after all. I was disappointed beyond words. I knew she had done it on purpose. I didn't have any proof, but a woman's gut feeling is never wrong. She had known we had made plans.

Mark begged for forgiveness. He said he would show me exactly how much I meant to him, how much he wanted us to work. The best part about it was the sex. Mark was extremely good at oral and never held back. In fact he loved oral sex and did not shy from trying new things to help spice up our relationship. This made our cosy nights in not only romantic, but exciting too. He loved scented candles and lingerie. I dressed up in sexy underwear for him, which made him excited; his eyes would light up. We used to go to different shops to find new outfits. Ann Summers was one of our favourites to explore together. He liked to try new things, new positions. A vibrating ring was certainly a new experience for me. I wasn't too keen, it didn't do anything for me. Nevertheless, Mark brought out a wild side to me. I became extremely daring, playful and erotic. The wilder we got, the greater the thrill and excitement.

On Valentine's Day Mark surprised me with a long-stemmed rose and a box of chocolates. The rose had a white stone in the centre. He took me out to dinner, which was so sweet of him. I loved the little details. The next surprise was a trip to Ann Summers where Mark drew my attention to a set of bondage toys: a pair of handcuffs, a long black-handled whip and blindfolds. They were all in my favourite colour – black. In some ways he reminded me of Edward. His eyes glowed and oh yes, we had to try it. It was new, it was exciting and had a different thrill to it. There was no spanking or lashing. We just played around with the idea of sex and fantasy.

Every relationship needs effort. Sex needs to be worked on or the excitement just wears off over time. But if you build a close bond, when the novelty of a new relationship fades and the physical attraction starts to diminish, the relationship turns into one of close friendship, mutual trust and understanding.

The negativity, which I overlooked in regard to Mark's personality, was that he loved money more than the average person. That too brought out a side to me which I never really appreciated. It made me arrogant, spoilt. I returned to a lifestyle which once I had experienced growing up, but had lost long ago. I did not like the changes resurfacing in me. Wanting him had made me change back to an older version of me. A me that I never liked.

Mark taught me that I just needed to be myself. Not to change for anyone, because it's just not worth it. There's no point in changing yourself at the cost of losing your identity and self-love.

No one could be as perfect as Edward; he was an exceptional partner. Apart from anything else, he was highly-skilled in the art of love making. His performance and the memory of him had been imprinted in the deepest, darkest parts of my soul. His touch had captivated my body and his mannerisms, enslaved my soul. Yet was he genuine? Not really. Edward was a ladies' man. If only he could have been a 'one man, one lady' type of gentleman.

The irony of the present situation? We continued to date. But men take a lot longer to mature than women. I wanted to break up with him on several occasions, but he begged me to continue and so I did. Finally, I stopped trying to break up with Mark. We were still together but I had decided to give him space because we had spent quite a lot of time together.

He had booked time off to be with me, but I insisted that he needed to catch up on his work. Mark's messages suddenly became fewer and farther between. I knew something was not right. He remained distant, but I gave him the benefit of the doubt. One day I received a text message saying we needed to talk and that it was about us. At that moment I knew, I was right from the very start. I went to meet him and we talked. He didn't want me to go back to his house with him, but I insisted. As soon as I walked in I spotted a brand-new television and table. His housemate was there, sitting at the table, watching the television. Had they bought them together?

Mark had sent me a picture of a little white side table for his room, which he had picked up from a second-hand shop. He had shared his excitement. But this big purchase? He hadn't even mentioned it. I knew the sudden change in behaviour had something to do with her. Mark went on to explain that it was over. He couldn't commit to me. He wanted a serious relationship but could not give me what I needed. I was puzzled. What was it that I needed?

All I wanted from Mark was commitment, nothing else. I just wanted to know that I meant something to him. He wasn't ready for a relationship or for anything serious, despite his proclamations otherwise. He was just a young man, easily manipulated by his housemate. All I could hope was that, one day, for his own sake, he would realise right from wrong. He lacked mental stability; I realised and took note of it. When I saw him the last time, as I collected my things, I let go of all my emotions and cried. I was angry at myself for not listening to my intuition and foolishly falling for his words. With every tear I cried, I healed. The break up broke me down completely because I longed for a steady, committed relationship. I wanted someone to call my very own, who would love and appreciate me. He seemed to share my aspirations, desires and ambition; he seemed to have the same passion and drive as I did to succeed, and a love of business. Yet our paths went down different routes. Perhaps because Mark had some unresolved feelings towards his ex? I walked away believing that he was too scared of getting hurt to enter into a meaningful relationship; he backed away before he actually started to feel for another person. Feeling meant risk; he could not handle getting close to someone; he could not bear the thought of getting hurt. He longed for a strong commitment but, in reality, he didn't know what he wanted.

The truth about human wants and desires is that the thought of getting something is often more exciting than getting what we actually desire. Some people appreciate the dream but can't handle the reality, they get disoriented.

That relationship left me broken. Mainly because I fell for the dream he promised, but not for the man himself. He was always talking about the future; things for us to do and places to visit, including family gatherings. But I was always wary of him. I did open up and share some personal information. I confided in him a little, but not completely. Although he seemed confident, it was a make believe, fake exterior for the outside world. Privately, he lacked confidence and self-esteem. The only stability he had was in his work.

Andrea Aviet

16th February- Healing from heartache.

I was broken. I needed to heal and let my feelings mend; it was hard work. The road to recovery, after my heart was broken and my dreams were shattered, took a little longer than anticipated. I knew that I had to be happy with in myself. If inner peace and acceptance of one's self is not there, you cannot truly accept others for who they are. It took a while but that was what led to the turning point in my life. That was the point at which, finally, my eyes opened. I began to recognise people for who they were. I could see through them, instead of relying on their sweet, misleading words.

Until this point, I could not see reality for what it was. I had been seeing the entire world, perceiving people as I thought they should be. I judged them according to my own rules. I learned the hard way that my outlook had been wrong. It had led me to heartache. Many times, a partner will show their true colours, but sometimes we overlook them, preferring to believe that they didn't really mean it. If a partner is serious in a relationship, they will do everything, try anything to make it work. We all chase after what we want and desire. Knowing how important you are to each other depends on entirely how much you both are willing to try to make it work.

I don't regret anything from my past. Each of my mistakes led to the becoming of the person I am today, and gave me insight into how different relationships are unique in their own way. Each partner taught me new strategies to cope and handle different situations. It was a good learning curve. Life is about experiencing, experimenting, discovering and learning.

Days and months passed. After looking over the messages I'd received from Mark, I decided to delete them all. Every e-mail, number, text, message. The day finally came when I was over him. No more pain, no more hurt, I was just happy to let go. Sadly, you can't keep something or someone who was never yours in the first place. Mark had spoken many beautiful words, no doubt with good intentions, but sadly I had fallen for them. Where was the action to support the words so eloquently spoken?

Andrea Aviet

20th February – Kate's revelation

At work the atmosphere was quite tense. The staff
loved to gossip and quite a few loved to slander. It's
true to say that a bad minority can often spoil it for
everyone. Let me, at this point, be totally blunt. A
friend pulled me to one side to tell me that my
name was right at the top of the gossip list at the
time. She spoke quiet sternly, even though we were
not that close. She said she wanted to let me know
what was being said about me. I appreciated her
honesty. There are not many people these days
who are open to such an extent. Neither do they
take the trouble to tell you about things which don't
really concern them. Most people are self-centred,
selfish and self-absorbed. I was shocked by what
she told me but I was pleased she had taken the
time to let me know. She gave me some good
advice and it all helped build, restructure and
accelerate the process of finding myself. This same
friend also kept trying to get me to go along with
her to her church.

She kept knocking on the door of my conscience,
hoping that I would one day go with her. With the
best of intentions, I would say yes and then end up
not going. Every Sunday, as it drew nearer, I
suddenly feel too tired. The long week had just
passed and I needed my rest. That's what I told
myself. This continued for a while until one day,

neither happy, nor convinced, I decided to give it a go. It was a small but welcoming crowd. They were kind and held their arms open to welcome any new comer into their place of worship. At the end of the ceremony they would have a little gathering over tea and coffee. It took a while but I eventually got used to it. Slowly but surely the struggle and mental battle between attending or resisting, ceased.

Simultaneously, I was changing. I was achieving more clarity in respect to goals that I could achieve, the direction I wanted my life to go in and dreams that I longed to fulfil. The gift of discernment was fully upon me. I was able to see people for who they truly were, and not be led astray.

The lady who introduced me to the church was beautiful. She was of average height , had a lovely personality and was bright and confident. She was the single mum of a beautiful little girl. I grew to know and understand her for who she really was and her inner strength and beauty far surpassed her outward looks. I made a shocking discovery in regard to Kate's life. If you looked at her from afar you would think she had not a worry in the world. But look more closely and something hugely worth of praise was uncovered. The more time we spent together, the more she revealed to me that being a single mother was not always easy. She had come out of a failed, abusive relationship and trying to survive with her little girl had led them both moving about a great deal. She had spent many hours travelling, packed in crowded trains with her daughter screaming that the crowds pushing against her body were hurting her. Yet Kate had found the strength to persevere, to be a source of strength and an inspiration for her little girl to follow. Hours of commuting between temporary homes, to work, school, church had meant they had missed many functions. There were many sacrifices made in the game of survival. Years of struggle had passed by. In the quest for a happy family life and love, she too had made plenty of mistakes: drugs, one-night stands, casual sex, lesbian clubs... She had tried everything and anything to be happy. Kate had been looking in all the wrong places for stability but finally she found herself, her inner peace and self-acceptance. She got her strength not only from being a mother and wanting the very best for her daughter, but also from changing her life entirely. She had turned to the church and had been filled with a truly happy inner peace and joy. Kate's church was a small Methodist church. It is said never judge anything based on size and truly I bear witness to the miracles I have seen amongst the few but dedicated. Kate's transformation, inner and outer glow, strength of character, focus, resilience and determination to combat every problem came from within. She was a self-reliant, strong young lady. But as she herself admitted, her strength came from this little group, their support and their enriched faith in God. I looked upon her as a good example.

Here was a gorgeous lady with no short-comings, yet she was alone. There was nothing about her which was unlikable or unlovable. Why was she still single? A question asked by many who met her.

Kate told me that if she wanted to, she could be in a relationship. It was not an issue for her to get a man. Men were always flirting with her, wanting her number, trying to impress her. All Kate desired was to find the *right* man. A man who would be right for her in every possible way. Not one who would try to pull her down, but rather uplift her and be her perfect other half. She was not willing to settle and would not give on finding her Mr Right.

Many of us women settle and that's where we go wrong. We don't go into a relationship with our eyes wide open and our mind free from pre-made notions and desires. But rather we jump in, head over heels. We rush in with our hearts ready in the palms of our hand, to be given over. Following Kate's example would definitely save a lot of us women, who are hopeless romantics, a lot of grief.

Quite a few months had passed and though there was no contact with Mark at the beginning it left me feeling empty. However now and then I recall random moments; his face and certain flash backs

Andrea Aviet

of him cooking or saying something to me. I was much stronger now. Time heals all. Slowly but surely, I was recovering from him. Perhaps the relapse of memory was just because of loneliness?

1st March – Sex and socialising

It was 5pm and Zack rang me. We are all going to the pub to have a drink and something to eat.

"Will you join us or are you going to stay by yourself, moping?"

Oh, that kind of invitation aggravated me.

I got to the pub a 7pm. It was crowded.

"We thought you were not going to make it as usual. Are you up for having some fun, or have you forgotten what fun feels like?" Zack shouted across the pub.

This line of questioning made me feel uncomfortable. Yet, I decided to stay because it had been a long time since I had been out in a lively environment. I wanted to hear music, have a few drinks, relax and chill out. Today was a day to loosen up and let my hair down...

Well I did enjoy the company and the food. It was all going well. After a few drinks the conversation took a turn, certain truths started to be revealed. When was the last time Zack had sex? If he could sleep with anyone who would it be and why? Zack was fair in complexion, with black hair and hazel eyes. His hair fell down to his jaw line and he usually tied it up. Since he was well-built he believed in wearing body hugging and revealing clothes. He knew how to get noticed. The conversation started to heat up. Mathew said he had gone out and had sex with a waitress in the toilet behind the pub. He really wanted to fuck her as she had a nice ass. Clare revealed that, under the influence of alcohol, she'd had a foursome, and although she could not recollect the events of the day, a video taken by one of the women involved revealed exactly how wild the night had really got. There was so much talk in regard to sex that even if you did not desire sex, you just started longing for it. At the end of the night, Zack said he would take me home, I could get a ride on his bike. I was a little worried about putting my arms around him after the long evening of sex talk. I was quite turned on and it wouldn't have been the first time I'd thought about having Zack in bed with me... would my fantasies become a reality this evening?

Well, he was, as I described earlier, irresistible, attractive, charming and he had a captivating personality. So it was a small spark of excitement that I climbed on to the back of his bike. The wine I'd drunk clouded my judgement slightly so I didn't realise how close I had sat to Zack. I pressed up tight against him pressing my breasts against his back. Zack asked if I was okay and truly, I was more than okay. When we got to my house he walked me to the door, helped me in and tried to kiss me goodnight. When I say he tried, he actually did kiss me goodnight.

Zack was very much like me in that beauty attracted us both. When he kissed me goodnight I reciprocated. We were soon at the point of no return. Zack reached round behind him and locked the door. He slipped off his shirt and told me he'd like to stay the night. Zack was a pleasure to be with. His stamina, his flow, his physique, all appealed to my senses. The way his fingers flowed all over my body. His gentle touch, the way he lifted my tiny waist and held it in his strong masculine arms. I loved feeling his smooth skin on mine. He held me tight and kept me close. Oh, the night was not nearly long enough for us as we lay under the white sheets; we couldn't keep our hands off each other all night. The difference between having sex with someone who is an amateur and someone who has a real talent, is like the difference between heaven and earth. The entire process is unrushed and gains momentum slowly, tantalisingly. We were so good together.

When daylight started to peer through my window I watched him sleep in my bed. Eventually he opened his eyes.

"Hi. Last night was great. I enjoyed it, what about you?"

Andrea Aviet

I could not help but laugh at him.

"We need to do this again, right?" He laughed.

Well I was not going to refuse. I had always had such a soft spot for him. He drew nearer and started to kiss me, playing gently with my breast with his long fingers. Feeling my response, Zack straddled me gently and penetrated deeply. We both grabbed the bars of the headboard and entered into the sex vigorously. Our efforts brought on orgasms from both of us and squeaks from the bed. The sheets fell off, pillows landed on the floor and Zack lay heavily on me. Extreme pleasure had left us both breathless, speechless for a while and pouring with sweat... it was a full-blown workout.

"Are you okay?" he asked.

"Yes, I'm good, just need to catch my breath."

We had to get ready and leave for the office. But when we walked into work together there were smiles all round. It was obvious from our behaviour that we had spent the night together. But we both knew it a one-off. Neither one of us was ready to commit to a serious relationship. Zack made it obvious he would like to get together again. But time and circumstance never allowed it to happen again.

10th March – A new chapter, secrets of love to discover

I wanted to understand the differences in relationships in order to get a better insight into why some relationships fail and some work well. Does religion and culture play a hand? Or is it forces beyond these that lead to certain relationships working out? Why is it that some women find wonderful men and still disrespect them by cheating once their back is turned? And why do so many of these same men remain faithful and full of love for their partner?

On the other hand, you have some ladies who are loyal, beautiful and trustworthy yet they end up with abusive and horrible men. It's like two sides of a coin attracting their direct opposites. Some couples are genuinely happy with a fairy tale ending and a life full of happiness. Then of course you have the singles who are ready to mingle, single parents who are definitely not ready to mingle but are happy, content with being by themselves, enjoying their own company. Finally, there are a few lesbian and gay couples whose relationships last for years. Why is it then that certain relationships end up in smoke? My new quest: to find answers about sex, relationships and how to get a love that will last, has meaning and has purpose.

Andrea Aviet

14th March - Love at 40

I met a lady through my work. She was very pleasant and had a good nature. We were to do a project together but instead of just being work acquaintances I could not help but become friends with her. Her skin was tanned, she a radiant smile, twinkling bright eyes and one of the friendliest souls I'd ever met. She was quite chatty and the conversation flowed as we got to know each other better. One of the things which stood out in particular was the glance that she gave me into her past. She was to be my first relationship lesson. Sandra had a partner. He was the father of her daughter but was not the kind of man a good woman should keep around. We exchanged our past storie. I told her about Mark and she was most sympathetic. The advice she gave me was crucially important. Move on. She explained that in her experience, men take a lot longer to mature than women. She had separated from her ex a while ago; the relationship was long over, not least because he had moved on to someone new and much younger. Sandra never wanted anyone to replace him. In fact, she resigned herself to turning 40 and being single. She didn't need anyone in her life. She worried about her age and that she might end up alone. That's when faith blessed her with a big surprise.

Sandra was parking her car in the office car park. As she walked towards the office she spotted Jake. He too had just parked his car; the attraction was undeniable and instantaneous. The connection was felt on both sides and sparks were flying. Sandra felt her heart leap and butterflies in her tummy. Who is to say love has any age limit? Love is precious and timeless. As the pair chatted and got to know one another, the feelings turned out to be mutual. The attraction grew over the next few days and they decided to meet up outside of work. They went for casual dates and learned more about each other every time they met. Jake had a son too. He had long been separated and was growing tired of meeting the wrong women. All he wanted at this point in his life was a good woman. That was the key factor: men take a lot longer to mature, which is why choosing the right woman is so important. In my experience, unless men have lived through heartbreak and loss, they will not grow up or face reality. Some men are so caught up with the illusion that they are forever young but fail to realise that the body ages and the youthfulness they feel is mental and emotional. Jake had grown up. He had long surpassed the phase of thinking he was young and dabbling at relationships. And his promises of long-standing relationships were not just words. He was actually ready to settle down. He knew exactly the level of commitment he wanted and was ready to give it back in return.

It was Sandra who actually drew to my attention that, what a man says and what he really wants or thinks, are entirely different. This revelation made me think of Mark. He had spoken of commitment, spending time together and about wanting a serious relationship. Yet he was not ready at all. He liked the thought of it all and that's as far as it went. Perhaps that is why I have always had doubts about entering a relationship with a younger man. They lack the level of maturity needed.

Sandra and Jake made a lovely couple and, over time, they bonded into a perfect family unit. Every couple has their ups and downs, their differences, but their relationship was mostly positive, most of the time. We sat laughing and talking about the fact that she had vowed to write a book about being single at 40, but how fate had something else in store for her. She had found true happiness at 40, proving that it is never too late to begin a new chapter in one's love life.

Their story gave me hope, inspiration and assurance. You never know what life will bring upon you nor how destiny will look down and smile at you. This was one happy couple who made it work for them.

17th March – Arranged marriages

I moved on to take a closer look at another lady in her sixties. She had been married for 40 years and was a decent lady and a mother to a young gentleman. Her son was well-educated and doing very well both professionally and personally. She had done exceptionally well to raise her son who was a dedicated, hard worker. So, I knew she would give her marriage the best she had to offer, that was just her nature. Curiosity got the better of me and I really wanted to find out what made her union last so long.

Rita seemed fine, but extremely negative. After long conversations with her, Rita told me that the marriage was arranged and was not a very happy one. She was an Asian lady and her religion and culture encouraged her to love, respect and look after her husband, no matter what he did. In her religion, once a daughter leaves her father's house after marriage, she belongs to her husband. He is the head of the family and provider of the household. Rita explained to me that she had suffered 40 years of mental and verbal abuse. But in the name of religion and family honour, there was no other option for her but to stay with him. The Asian culture is such that if the marriage suffers a breakdown, so does the family honour. Rita explained to me that while her son was growing up she thought it best to be quiet and live peacefully for his sake. After all these years had passed, she feared that she would not be able handle a new start, a new life by herself. Sadly, it was easier for her to stay in an unhappy marriage and carrying on as normal.

It always surprises me that, in a world of modern technology, advancing thought processes, scientific and medical breakthroughs, that mankind still remains backward-looking when it comes to religion, culture and family honour. It reminded me of the dark ages. There was no way I could help Rita unless she was willing to break away from her old engraved thought process and start anew.

19th March – The Karma Sutra

Rohit was a lovely man and a good friend of mine. He'd been brought up in the Asian culture but was quite different from Rita's husband. He belonged to a well-to-do family, where respecting parents and their wellbeing was given priority above all other things. Rohit wanted to succeed and had natural drive, intelligence and passion. He was a great believer in setting goals and targets for himself, and always put a time limit on them, which forced him to work hard to achieve his goals.

Rohit was tall and slim. So was his wife. She was also friendly and beautiful. But they hadn't chosen one another. Their marriage was arranged. Rohit's wife had been chosen for him by his parents. The marriage was fairly new and they were both willing to work hard at it. They hadn't lived together before they were married, so they worked hard at understanding each other's natures and compromising as much as they could. He was a good husband and father, always providing for his family. Rohit was also a dedicated son.

As good friends, we shared a lot of personal things between us. Rohit always wanted to understand the mind of a woman. He would often ask me for advice. I would frequently do his shopping for birthdays, anniversaries and special days, and he would give what I had bought to his wife. She was very happy that he thought about her. Sometimes it takes a woman to know a woman. Rohit always thought about her though, from smallest to the biggest of things. Her happiness was important to him; he respected the fact that she was the mother of his child, that she cooked for him and looked after the entire household.

In order for a relationship to be a healthy, it has to be a two-way street. Of giving and taking equally on both sides. Rohit gave financially, his wife ran the household. But there were huge drawbacks to the marriage in the bedroom.

In my experience, women in the east are not as sexually open as they are in the west. Their culture, family values, upbringing, ethics and religion teach them that extrovert behaviour is wrong, therefore they shy away from it. Rohit's wife, Shetal, was a good friend of mine and called me sister. She wanted some advice from me and of course I was more than happy to oblige. She felt uncomfortable with experimenting sexually, trying new styles and exploring techniques of love making. Her upbringing had left her with a lack of openness towards such matters, and made her awkward, even her own husband. I asked her if she had ever read the Kama Sutra. She said she hadn't, so I advised her she ought to. The Kama Sutra, regarded as the bible of sexual positions and art of love making, has its roots buried in the ancient Asian world itself. There is so much to learn from this insightful book on sex. Sex is just not getting naked when you feel horny. It's so much more; a skilful art to elevate each other's soul, boost your energy levels, build a bond through love and learn how to satisfy your every need. I have heard that when you bond, the souls bond too. Why is it you feel close to your partner? Simply put, he leaves his essence and part of himself within you after you have slept together. Also known as "**soul ties**". Sadly, not many get the right understanding of the phrase. It's not wise to sleep around with multiple partners as they will all end up leaving traces inside of you.

There were so many different positions for Shetal to try. The Erotic Accordion, The Pinwheel, Electric Slide, Arch de Triomphe, Bootyful View, Ladder Loving, Lap Dance and Leg Up were just a few to start with.

Shetal had no need to feel embarrassed. I could understand why she shied away but, as I tried to advise her, doing the same thing over and over again can get boring. One can't eat the same food for breakfast, lunch and dinner for three consecutive days without being absolutely fed up with the repetition. She loved cooking so I thought a food analogy would give her a better understanding.

Rohit always seemed to fail to understand the mind of a woman. He understood her heart but not her desires. He understood her wants but not all of her physical needs. We had the most beautiful conversation over dinner at their house, a few days after I introduced Shetal to the Kama Sutra. I asked some questions which I would not dare to ask others, if we did not have that level of closeness.

Can you guess what I asked?

"Rohit, my friend, do you love Shetal?"

"Of course I do, what kind of a silly question is that?"

"Well, how much do you love her? And do you love all of her?"

"I do."

"Tell me, how do you make her feel special?"

"I work hard, I provide for her and buy her whatever she wants."

Perhaps I was being too subtle. I was trying to steer the conversation towards their sexual relationship. I wanted to know about it. Every detail of their intimacy. How did he make her feel? Did he go down on her? Did he ravish every part of her body and show her exactly what she meant to him? Did she feel appreciated, as a woman should be?

We had an insightful talk. I told Rohit that a man who satisfies his lady fully will never lose her, and will have no need to worry about competition or unfaithfulness. Make love to her, don't just have sex. Show her how much you care, be gentle.

I'd noticed, while we were waiting for our dinner, that he had tried to grab her while she was setting the table and she hadn't appreciated it. Men are so different from women. I specifically brought that up while we spoke. Rohit was embarrassed. He couldn't believe that I spotted him. Yet, I had to share my thoughts with him.

I challenged him to imagine the scene I was going to set for him. He told me I was silly for wanting to play mind games. So, I bet him £20 that I could make him get an erection and leave him wanting to have sex with his wife. The bet was on. He was very excited to play a game that he thought he was definitely going to win. That was not going to happen.

"Rohit have you ever looked at Shetal's neck and felt like kissing it? Imagine running your tongue down the side of her neck, further down and exploring her fully while you do it. I want you to remember that your hands must be busy too. So, reach down and feel her smooth legs. Her skin is soft like butter, she responds to your gentle touch. With your mouth I want you to gently move down further her body. Find her belly button and kiss it. Notice her hips and the way they curve, look at her slim waste. If only you could turn her round, hold her firmly, and push yourself in from behind. If only she was open to it, you could take her right now, over the kitchen counter. Now I want you to notice the way her eyes glow when she's happy, feel her warm breath on your shoulders when you're on top of her, her nails digging into your back. Can you take her while she calls out your name, begs you not to stop? Can you handle it?"

"Tell me more" he responds, excitedly.

"Well before you undress her, while you kiss her luscious red plump lips, you must do something special. Before you suckle her breasts, you must go down first. I want your hand to play within the warmth of her vagina, let your fingers work their magic, let her feel you're not in a rush, but you're taking your time. Let her know you want it slow. That's how a woman likes it. Now can you see her stopping you? I'm sure she loves the attention; I am sure she loves what you're doing to her. If she pushes your hands and sighs, don't worry. Carry on. As the sighs grow louder and she digs her nails into your hands you know, you have done something right.

"Don't stop. Gently move round the back of her and, with your other hand, glide over her breasts. Gently rub and caress her. Her breasts are youthful, soft and beautiful; ravish them lovingly. She does not stop you because while you play with her she is being satisfied and submits to your every will. When you know she is yours, completely surrendered, undress your prize and take her from behind."

"Oh my God I am hard; can you please go so I can try it with Shetal."

I'd won the bet.

I told him to calm down and start from the beginning again. I didn't want to cause any problems between the two of them. If Shetal saw him in his present state after talking to me she might get the wrong idea. No wife, I guess, would be happy to be walking in on their man with an erection after talking to another woman, even if it was for their own benefit. The next day, Rohit called me and thanked me. They had both enjoyed the evening and it was the best sex he'd had since the day they got married. The rest of my advice was for Shetal to practise. A couple must work together and try to excite themselves, together. Reciprocate and be ready to give to each other in all ways. Satisfy each other.

Andrea Aviet

Being a good wife does not solely mean taking care of the house or being a good mother. You have to be a good partner to your man too. People sometimes fail to understand the importance of keeping their man sexually satisfied. Sex makes up a big part of any relationship.

I am sure Shetal got my point. In fact, I also asked her, why do women wear different lingerie with different textures and designs? It's not just to excite their partner, but also to accessorise their natural beauty, to feel good and to look good. I gave Shetal every possible piece of advice I could think of. Now it was up to her. She had a good man. Now she had to work out how hard she was willing to work for their relationship. Was she willing to go that extra mile?

Every culture has their positives and negatives. In the west, women seem to decide to get rid of their men as often as they would a bra. At least they don't stand for any nonsense in the name of culture. But this directly impacts on divorce rate. Women in the west live with greater protection in terms of human rights. But living in the west does not make you a westerner if, ideologically, you belong to the east. In the east the rate of separation and divorce is a lot lower, mainly because of the restrictions of religion culture. Hopefully, Shetal had learnt something from the advice I gave her.

Opaque Desires

Lack of openness, confidence and experience were the only real issues they faced as a couple.

Andrea Aviet

3rd April – Dress to impress

On my birthday, Kate and I decided to go out for dinner. She insisted that I needed a break, some time to relax. So, she organised a girl's night out together, with dinner and wine, in central London. We went to a lovely Spanish restaurant and just enjoyed each other's company. We indulged ourselves with good food, we relaxed, we talked, we laughed. We were two ladies having a good night out. I drew Kate's attention to the two couples sat on either side of us. There seemed to be strange parallels between them. Both men had evidently made an effort to look good for a dinner date. They were both smart but understated. The ladies, on the other hand, had made zero effort to look good. They were dressed casually, as if they had just thrown something on.

"That's another drawback of the long-term relationship," I explained to Kate. "The comfort zone." Women make the effort to look their very best when they are trying to attract someone's attention. Perhaps they've just broken up with a partner and are trying to make themselves look brand new, to attract a new partner. When we want to, we women will take an interest in what we wear, our makeup can be flawless, jewellery well-selected. And of course, the seductive high heels to give us that extra height and make our legs look longer and sexier.

But with the passing of time, as we get into a relationship, we start to take the relationship for granted. We get to comfortable, laid back, and we start to slide and let go of ourselves. Why? Because we think we are a couple. There's no need to maintain the effort. Many women think, once they have a good man, that's it. "My man's not going anywhere now."

Well I have some questions for you. Are you sure about your man? How sure are you? Would you bet your life on him? I only ask because that's what you commit to. A large part of your life being given over to him. You give your time, commitment, togetherness. These are some important questions for you to ask yourself when it comes to your relationship.

But there is no rational excuse for women to become laid back like this. There are many single women out there and not enough of good men. Today, as the world stands, most people desire what someone else has. The desire to get someone else's man becomes more attractive sometimes. So, what are you giving your man to look at? A plain Jane?

Andrea Aviet

Observe, the next time you're walking down the high street; you will see people of different shapes and sizes, different styles of dressing. First impressions count for an awful lot. In that split second while you're rushing around, the one thing you notice is the look of someone. How handsome or beautiful does someone look? First it's the face you notice, then the clothes. If time permits a conversation, verbal interactive skills come down the list at third, at best. If you're not attracted to the way a person looks, that's the start of a no-go area. There's no chemistry, no attraction.

Going back to the restaurant, both men were continuously looking at me and Kate; we held their attention. We were simply dressed but we had the heels, the makeup, the look and the charm. The combination of the look, and sparkling personalities to go with it, was unbeatable. Those ladies were nothing in comparison to us. I would not like to have my man's interest continuously wandering over to the table beside us, if I were in their position.

If I were in a relationship, I would keep working at it and wanting my partner to work with me, on us.

People need to look good for themselves and for each other. The act of dressing smartly and looking good has so many positive points. Not least, others appreciating the way you look. Knowing that a stranger likes the way you look can give you a confidence boost. It can also help with spicing up your very own relationship. Taking pride in one's self is always a good thing. Kate commented, once we left, that she could not understand why someone would come for dinner without making an effort. All I can say is that we had a lovely time and enjoyed ourselves. We were definitely dressed to kill!

Andrea Aviet

16th April – Sex for entertainment

Simon and Laura were always into each other; they seemed happy, jovial and very much in love. But as with all things, looks can be deceiving. Their relationship was complicated. From the outside, a relationship can seem perfect, yet you're observing from afar. When I got a closer look at them guess what I stumbled upon?

Well their form of entertainment was each other's company. Now, let me go into further details to explain to you their circumstances. Simon loved children and was a computer technician by profession. He had a very strong character and held very steadfast opinions. He wasn't one for taking orders. He loved to live by his own rules and do as he pleased.

Then Simon met Laura.

Laura was a young lady who had been divorced from her first husband. She had her son at an early age. Simon had children from a previous relationship too, although he had never been married. They thought they were a perfect couple. I was very happy for them because I felt Laura had found someone nice. Simon loved sex. He knew how to treat his woman in the bedroom, was a good father and loved their kids. But was he a good partner? Being a good lover and father does not make you a good partner.

No one is perfect. I understand that. But surely you have to be able to live with a partner? To tolerate their foibles?

Simon liked to control Laura. She was still young, but Simon would not allow her to wear any makeup; he did not like it. And she wasn't allowed enjoy herself. Giving her heart over to Simon without making any ground rules was one of the worst mistakes Laura ever made. She changed the way she dressed, she changed the way she behaved, what she ate and where she went. Briefly she moulded herself into the woman he wanted her to be, not the woman she was. She bore his children too because he wanted them, not because she desired to have them. Every part of her, she gave to him. He was a sta- at-home dad, while she worked all the hours of the day to bring food in, to provide for the family, and to pay the bills. I could see unhappiness in her eyes. The pressure of her life was making her crack. What was wrong with this couple?

I knew that all was not as it seemed in her relationship. I advised her she needed to find time for both of them. They needed to be together, alone. They were both struggling with all their children and too much stress. She worked long hours, leaving Simon to cope with the children on his own, for many hours of the day. When she returned home, that was his time to relax and have a break. He would do the housework while she was at work. They were always apart, so where was the togetherness?

I advised Laura that family time is always necessary. Life is stressful, and having a large family adds to the stress if it's not handled properly. And couples should never forget that everyone needs 'me time'. Simon and Laura also needed 'together time'.

Sadly, my fears for them came true. I heard the family had broken down; Laura had walked out on the kids and her partner. A horrible and terribly sad situation.

People judge from an outside perspective, but we can never truly know what's going on behind closed doors and between different couples.

Everyone has ups and downs. We all cope with our own stresses and trials. How we deal with it, the measures we put in place, determine the path our lives take. Perhaps if they'd put some money aside for a professional baby sitter, gone out for dates, arranged candle lit dinners, their relationship might have been very different. His attitude might have changed and she could have released some of the pressure she was under.

We must each find our own way. What works for one does not necessarily work for another. I hope, for their family's sake, when they have had time to sort out their differences they can find their own way. Whether as a couple or as individuals. But perhaps they can work together to be strong for their children, even if they remain on their separate paths.

Life is not a bed of roses, as the saying goes. There are many thorns amongst the roses and what we need is to remember is that, once we pass through that level of hardship, life will get easier. We can't give up; everything has to be worked upon, slowly but surely.

Happiness cannot be bought; it must be developed and worked upon. I would encourage everyone to work on happiness. To work on themselves. If you like music, listen to it. If you love to read pick up a book. You must find some 'you time' and do what works for you.

Many people seem unable to separate time and relationships. They mix everything up, which causes a big muddle. Even as part of a couple, each individual still needs their own space and time. Time to relax by themselves, unwind and do what they love to do. Whether that time is spent dancing, hanging out with friends, going to the gym, it doesn't matter. There's no reason why both can't do the same things simultaneously. It all comes down to organisation of time. Our lives are so busy. It's like a rat race, but if we don't find time for what's important to us, then who will? I don't want life to just pass me by, working only to pay bills and survive. I want my dreams to be fulfilled. Or at least I try to fulfil them.

Making time, scheduling a plan and sticking to it really helps in achieving what we desire.

Many times, I've seen partners content to cling to each other and stay away from others. There are several reasons for this. If it's a young romance, just starting out, they want to spend time exploring each other. Sometimes it can be that one partner is insecure about the other. Lack of self-confidence can often lead to one partner now wanting to spend time apart from the other; uncertainty can lead to insecurity and possessiveness. This can suffocates the relationship at a very early stage, even before it can blossom. The best way to avoid this pitfall is to give each other space. If someone is not true and was never yours it does not matter what you do, they will still never be yours.

1st May – Love, jealousy, possessiveness

Sally fell in love with Evan. Sally was young and beautiful. Evan was an ambitious young man, progressing very fast in his career. He'd worked hard. He'd climbed up from rock bottom and was now reaching for the higher management level in his chosen profession. Evan wanted to keep rising. He was mature enough to know that he needed to stay focused on his career, but he lacked that maturity personally when it came to commitment and having a relationship. He wanted a girlfriend but was not ready to settle down. Sadly, Evan had to let go of Sally. She became too anxious, too possessive and due to fear of losing him started wanting commitment in the form of a family, marriage and children. Sally tried to rush them into marriage, not giving them time to grow together. Her over eagerness caused negative reactions from Evan. Evan wasn't looking for commitment and marriage and children.

That's sadly how many relationships end. They lack patience and an understanding of each other's needs. Dreams are not respected goals are not achieved. Encouraging each other selflessly helps strengthen the present relationship and build a strong foundation for the future together. Sally's impatience caused such a deep wedge that the relationship broke down. It was not Sally's fault. Nor was it Evan's. He wanted to bring his dreams into reality, whereas she dreamt of a family life and commitment without even thinking about financial stability. 'Puppy love', I call it. Yes, how many of us remember making the same mistakes? Losing something good because we were in too much of a rush to get that special level of commitment? When do you captivate that special someone's heart?

It's not only the physical attraction which makes a relationship work. Although that can be hard to believe, since we live in a materialistic world. But it is the inner beauty that strengthens relationships. What makes you stand out from the rest and makes you special?

There's competition all around. How do you stand out? What do you do to make yourself happy within a relationship? Being confident in one's self is a big turn on. It causes a glow around you and just makes you more visible; it sets you apart from all others. It helps you lead instead of being led. There's something very appealing in finding your own inner strength and standing on your own two feet.

6th May – Relationship illusion

Nikki was a small lady; she dressed well and carried herself in a dignified manner. She needed no one and looked for no one's company. She was confident, an eloquent speaker, and had a charming character. She believed in one principle: either you love me for me or you don't. Either way, she was not about to change for anyone. She always said she was just happy being her. That's the best way to be. In many relationships we try to change the other person. Sometimes we see something we really don't like in the person. But we decide to overlook it and psychologically start telling ourselves it's not too bad, that we can change what we don't like in the person. My advice would be, don't fool yourself. Spare yourself disappointment, fights, aggravation, disagreements and arguments. It's not worth it. If you plan to start a relationship, start it for the right reason and with the right person. When you start to think 'Okay he's a smoker, I don't like that but I can change that about him once we get serious about each other' you're entering into a fool's game. Your new partner could have had this habit for a number of years. It could help release their tension, be a bad habit or an addiction. You could be accused of making something small into a big issue, of changing your mind about it ('It wasn't an issue when we first started dating'). Or you could be accused of trying to be controlling; they will not be able to comprehend the sudden change in your behaviour.

In a new relationship we are all on our best behaviour. We are trying to create a good impression and getting to know each other. Every action and behaviour is measured and planned. The clothes, the shoes, the perfume or aftershave... But very often this doesn't reflect our true selves. Honestly, if you tell someone right from the start what you expect, your likes, your dislikes, it could save you both a lot of time. Playing the fool's game only leads to wrong judgements and regrets once the novelty of the new relationship starts to get stale. An open, honest relationship is always the best way forward.

Many relationships break down because people can't truly accept one another for who they really are. I don't believe people hide. We show our partners everything about ourselves, eventually, but you just have to be vigilant and recognise signs when they occur.

Cherry was engaged to Nathan. They had been dating for three years and had been through several break ups. They always got back together. Cherry wanted Nathan to give up drinking. They would argue a lot and Cherry would say she'd had enough. She'd get mad with him for not doing as she asked. One day, at a friend's dinner party, Nathan had a bit too much to drink. It made Cherry angry because she hated seeing him stumble around and make a fool of himself. The embarrassment of having friends judging them and commenting that he could not hold his drink was too much to bear. She knew there would be gossip the next day that again it was him who broke something in his drunken state. I could understand why she got upset. All she ever requested was for Nathan to drink in moderation so that he wouldn't behave that way. Every time he managed to disappoint her. Nathan contacted her the next morning via text. He apologised and once promised he'd never do it again. But it wasn't the first time. How many occurrences must happen before an end is put to things?

As usual, Cherry forgave him because, in spite of everything, she really loved him. She always said he was a loving person with a generous spirit, when he was sober.

A few years later I met Cherry in the supermarket. She was shopping with her adorable daughter. I asked about Nathan and she replied we are no longer together. They had separated. He visited every weekend to see his little girl. I felt sad for them all. The little girl had a single mum and a part-time dad. Cherry, on the other hand, had so much in her favour. She was young and intelligent. Sadly her judgement was clouded by her affections for Nathan. Did he hide who he was? Did he pretend to be someone else? All the answers to those questions are 'no'. He had always showed her his true nature. If only she had been strong enough to walk away from her disappointment earlier, she might not have had to be raising the little girl on her own, now.

It isn't always easy doing the right thing. In most cases it takes lots of courage and hard work. She was so afraid of being alone; she wanted to be loved by someone even though they might not have been right for her. After years of seeing him drunk, why did she think after getting married he would change? The point I am trying to emphasise is that you can't change someone. You either accept them for who they are, or you walk away.

Fear of loneliness is such a concern amongst people today that they will hold on to anyone. Why not be content within yourself and be happy, confident enough to know you don't need anyone else?

I really do think that most of the time we crave things, even though we see it's not right for us.

So, we settle for the idea, choosing to ignore the reality. That's why so many relationships breakdown. We get fed up of picking up the pieces, fed up of trying and overlooking certain things until the entire situation gets so frustrating and out of control that we can no longer tolerate each other.

9th May – Love or fear

I'm a people-watcher. I watch passers-by. I watch people wherever I can.

At first glance, a couple walking hand in hand may look amazing together. But first glances can be deceiving. Misleading impressions can be gained this way.

Here's an example.

He looks so protective and caring. He holds her close and towers over her. She looks up at his face, watches him closely and being alert to everything he does and says? She is beautiful; she is elegant, quiet and aloof. Why is she so proud of herself, why does she walk around with so many airs and graces? Why does she have so much pride? Is it her lifestyle or is it her lover?

But look closer. All may not be as it seems. She is far from free, she's trapped. Far from happy, she's miserable. Far from looking lovingly at her partner, she's actually fearfull of him. She watches his every move keenly. Does she really love him or is she more terrified?

This particular relationship was odd. I had noticed this couple before, and something did not seem right. From afar we can all sometimes covet someone else's life. But just because they project a certain lifestyle, it isn't necessarily true. I heard people pass comments about how lovely a couple they were, always together, always side by side.

But I had my suspicions. Sometimes she'd disappear for a while and then reappear without warning. One day my suspicions were confirmed and he ended up giving her a black eye. Yes, that's right, a black eye. He was a violent man with a nasty temper. That's why she watched him carefully, so she would know when to protect herself.

The grass always looks greener on the other side, doesn't it?. So many of us woman long to be in a relationship. We all want to belong to someone, but at what cost? Not every partner is a good partner, and not every relationship is a match made in heaven.

Are we willing to pay any price to be with someone else? Stop and think. Don't be miserable because you're alone. Be happy and content to know your true worth. Never envy that which you don't have. Sometimes it's better not to have than to have someone who will make your life a living hell.

Sadly, in the world today, we seem to be getting even more jealous and more envious.

Personally, I don't want a relationship that just looks good from the outside. I'd rather it looked like nothing special but in reality, was everything I wanted it to be. My happiness counts more than anything else and stability, along with peace of mind, is more important to me. When you're happy within yourself you can achieve greatness, reach new heights. A happy home and a happy environment are most important.

You should come home to a partner who understands and comforts you, rather than stresses you out.

Why do we get into a relationship?

Relationships are not meant to fill a void. Rather they're meant to grow a bond of togetherness, love, mutual respect. Relationships should help both partners, build each other up. That would be a relationship which I would be very happy to have, one which helped us grow and develop together. Behind every successful man is a woman. That's the saying. But I prefer the saying 'behind every successful couple lies the love and support of each other'.

What makes a relationship stand out?

I have seen so many of us women not really giving ourselves a chance at finding a relationship that works. It's not easy to find one like that but let time pass, don't rush to make rash decisions, know what you want and who you want. That will help you find the right man. Many of us don't know our own mind. We think we want a man because he dresses well, looks smart and respectable. But what about the rest of his qualities? One has to look at the entire picture to get a better understanding. Would you be happy with a smoker if smoke affects you? When choosing your perfect partner, I think it's important to firstly understand your own needs and requirements. What do you want? Is it a casual relationship? Is it friends with benefits? Is it a serious relationship with commitment? Or is it a one-night stand? Knowing your own mind will help you map out what kind of a man you want.

Here's a simple exercise. Take a sheet of paper and write down your needs and expectations from a partner. Then write in a comparison column what his nature and behaviour is like. Tick the ones which coincide. Now ask yourself by carefully looking at the rest, left unticked, can I live with a person like this? It's most important to be an honest and fair judge while evaluating the decisions, don't cheat yourself. If you feel you can't go ahead, then don't. It's never too late to change your mind.

12th May – Sex addiction

James had not a care in the world. At 37, he was a father to three boys from three different women. He was a very nice person, but his biggest problem was womanising. When he was with a woman he would give his all, be very devoted. Yet as soon as he left her house and was out of her arms, he'd throw himself straight into arms of the next lady he saw. He was addicted to sex. Sometimes multiple partners were still not enough for him, and he wanted more. A friend of mine was head over heels in love with him. This is when it gets tricky, especially since you don't plan to fall in love with someone. She insisted what she felt for him was real love. Mary was keen to stress that he made her feel so special and went into great details.

James was tall, slim and muscular. He had a polite yet charming personality. He was open and friendly. He never lied. He told woman who he got involved with that they were not the only ones he was dating at that given time. But he was exceptionally good in bed. That's what I heard from Mary, who could not stop herself from singing his praises. She went clubbing with him one night after work. When they got to his place, with the intention of getting changed and heading out, James wild self just took over; he helped Mary undress and gave her the best sex of her life. He had sex with her all night long and still didn't seem to tire. In Mary's words there was no stopping him. She could not believe his energy levels nor could she believe how long he could keep going without coming. She said he was too good to pass up and just craved him. He was better than her vibrator. She did not know much about him, yet she desired him. Mary characterised her feelings as being in love, yet when I questioned her it was instantly clear that she was too young and could not distinguish between her own feelings of love and lust.

Have you ever been dressed up, looking your best to go out for dinner with a special gentleman who just stands out to you? He manages to capture your attention even in a room filled with other people. Glances pass between you both, eyes interlock and a smile is exchanged. That's his sign. He approaches you as your heart races you can't help but wonder will his conversation do his sex appeal any justice?

After the first five minutes of conversation you realise, oh yes, he has the entire package. He is not crude but polite, not shy but bold. He has a certain quality which just draws you in and keeps your interest going. Something about him is mesmerising. The way he smiles captivates you. You start to desire him, you long for his touch. You imagine his arms around you and you start to wonder what it would be like to have him now, and feel him close. What would he be like in bed? How would he look without his clothes on? What lies beneath? You want him right now, as your craving starts to increase. You wonder, what can you do to stay in control? As you spend time in simple conversation over a glass of wine you want to leave. Your feelings are becoming uncontrollable. You can't just go up to him and kiss him. You're a lady. You cannot voice your opinion and your lustful desire.

So instead you politely get up saying you need to leave. He walks you out, reaches to kiss you goodbye on the cheek. But instead, you reciprocate and your lips become locked, tongues intertwined, that's the sign he was waiting for. That's no ordinary first-time kiss, he gets his hint, a silent go-ahead. He smiles, offers to drive you. The two of you leave together and the night is yours to claim. Driven by lust, ignited by passion, a long, sweaty, wild night is about to gear up.

That's lust; uncontrollable, overwhelming desire to have someone based on sudden impulse because you long for them. It's not love, it's not permanent, it's all in that moment of time. Savage, impulsive love-making. He drives you to his place. With wild desire and raging hormones you just follow like a little lustful lamb. Luckily, he is a decent man. But he can't resist you either. He doesn't take advantage, but rather a gentle lead.

"Would you like a drink" he asked. "How can I help make you comfortable?"

He pours a glass of red for you to share under the dim lights. As you sipy our wine he leans in and kisses you, from cheek to neck, from collar bone to chin. He said all he desired from the moment his eyes fell upon you was to taste your lips. As you kiss it feels like the entire room grows brighter. This is one of the most exciting nights you have lived through. His gentle touch, embrace, the way he led you to the bedroom, so romantically, by handing you a single white flower. You're clueless about where he got it from but the gesture was graceful, stylish, elegant. There's a vast difference between a man who desires you, yet takes his time, and a man who just rushes to jump into bed with you.

Having been in both situations, I can tell you that both are one-night stands, yet the first situation leaves you more fulfilled as a woman who has been appreciated, as opposed to a woman who has been used.

Mary had no clue what love was. She thought she was in love. But James was a play boy, in love with the idea of being loved, satisfying multiple woman and in return not only getting their devotion but being showered with expensive gifts. The list of devoted playmates seemed to grow each month. The phrase 'one woman, one man' meant nothing to James. Mary's misguided thoughts and conclusions were based upon how nice he was to her, how polite he was and how great the sex was. So it had to be love. It could not possibly be anything else.

Andrea Aviet

5th June – Unexpected love

When does true love strike? It has no special moment, time, place or person. Sometimes, you just have a good life but it can be lonely without that someone special.

'The One' does not come in a special package. A friend of mine loves to tell the story of how he met his perfect other half on a school trip. After many girlfriends who were not appropriate, she was the one he would never have chosen or thought of settling down with.

He liked excitement; he liked his women to be fit and capable of doing lots of things. He pursued many women who fell into his 'perfect package', yet it was those relationships which just broke down as fast as they started. The excitement fizzled out quite early in the relationship. As soon as that happened it lead to break down.

What made her so special is that their eyes did not captivate each other's interest at first glance. She was a hidden treasure. Let me explain. Hendry was going on a school trip with his niece. He was helping his sister, a single mother of one. She had to work and could not get the time off, but little Kate wanted someone to go with her to the beach. Hendry was asked if he could accompany her. This, he remarked, was fate. Hendry was a good uncle to his niece; he played with her, did the occasional stint babysitting when he could. He was very busy being a young, upcoming barrister. His work took up a lot of time, commitment and dedication.

He always thought his perfect match would be a female barrister. One who he could communicate with and discuss all the dealings of the day. However, life had a little surprise for him. They say no good deed goes unnoticed and nothing in life happens without a reason. That Friday morning Hendry went to school with Kate. Everyone thought he was Kate's dad because they got on so well. He was brilliant with her. The teaching assistant, Annabel, was kind and softly spoken. She had blue eyes and delicate features, with waist-long, thick black hair. She could literally turn a bad situation into a good one with her smile, such was her personality. However, Hendry took no notice of her at first. In his opinion, teaching was a boring job. Nothing exciting happened in teaching. Annabel and Hendry started talking during the trip. Something triggered his interest in her, although he never quite understood what; it baffled him as to why he was drawn to her. He told Annabel that he was Kate's uncle and they chatted amiably for the rest of the trip. He mustered the courage to ask her if she would like to go for a coffee with him, just so that they could talk some more. He was a man who knew, if he wanted something, he had to work for it. He wanted to get to know her so.... he invited her out. She agreed and they exchanged numbers.

Finding common time to fit each other's busy schedules proved to be a little problematic. London life is often busy and manic. If you're not looking for a one-night stand, but rather something more meaningful, it becomes quiet challenging. After lots of planning and time management, Hendry and Annabel finally got to have their coffee together. Hendry discovered that his interest was completely justified. She had many talents and her own father was a judge. She had studied law but did not find any fulfilment in the profession, so she decided to become a teaching assistant instead. She felt very content shaping the lives of young children. Hendry could not help but smile. First impressions could be very misleading.

Their relationship flourished, and one day, they decided that they would both like to commit to each other and go to the next level. Hendry gave me goosebumps as he related their chance meeting, took me through their love journey and then told me about the romantic proposal he had made to her. Annabel was quite cross one day. She explained that she felt sidelined by Hendry's career for the past few months. This was a problem for her because, as a young girl, she had watched her mother wait and wait patiently for her father's affection. Every day he would come home, too tired to talk, and ignore his doting wife. She had seen how the law profession had taken its toll upon their family life. The potential for this to happen to her and Hendry worried her a great deal. In an attempt to cheer her up, Hendry had arranged a romantic getaway. Three nights in a hotel with sightseeing included. To her amazement, on the second night Hendry made a toast to the rare treasure he had found, and thanked her for being an important part of his life. As Annabel sipped her glass of champagne, a ring floated towards her lips. She could not believe her eyes. It was a diamond engagement ring. All of a sudden, the lights became dim in the restaurant, the violinist played music and walked slowing in their direction. Hendry took the ring out of the glass held it in his hand.

He proposed with the words: "Will you marry me and make me the happiest man alive?"

"Yes," she replied, teary-eyed.

She could not say anything more as she was so caught up with emotion.

Their relationship, to date, has with stood the test of time. Since then they have had a little girl of their own and Kate is very excited when she gets to play big sister to uncle Hendry's daughter.

Hendry's advice for me to pass on to others is this. Don't judge someone by the way they look, because who knows where or when you will find your other half. Keep an open mind because true love does not come well-labelled, and once the opportunity is lost, you never know how long it will take to get another chance at true happiness.

I found his advice simple but wise. This could only come from a man who has loved, lost, had his heart broken and survived a broken relationship. In Hendry's words what a man actually says he wants and what he really wants are entirely different. The secret to winning a man's heart is to set him free to be himself and give him space, so you both can grow together. When a man feels he has to hide, can't be free, can't be himself, he does not want to be around you anymore. The tighter your grip, the more he suffocates and the easier it is for him to walk away.

Men are born hunters. Let your man loose to hunt and he'll chase after you. Never chase behind a man, that's the worst mistake. Hold your own, be your own woman and find your own path.

8th July – Female sexuality and empowerment

Mel was sweet. She was young, blonde and Russian. She had an aggressive air about her and she would not let anyone get close to her.

"Why is it that you get so rude and nasty when any man approaches you, just to hold a simple conversation?" I asked Mel.

She sighed and then after a few moments of silence said, "Every man who has approached me has done so not because they wanted to get to know me but rather because they are only interested in sleeping with me."

I smiled at Mel. "It's hard being beautiful, right?"

Mel looked puzzled. I smiled again and complimented her. "Take a look around. There are many women who would love to walk in your shoes. There are many women who would like to be as beautiful as you." I explained. "So many women don't understand their own assets and how to work them properly. Some have a large bust, some a large behind, others may not have either yet they might be very pretty, delicate and petite in appearance. Each one of these women can accessorise their assets and turn that into a tool to achieve a goal."

Andrea Aviet

Mel resented it when men approached her because of her beauty. I gave Mel the example of her friend, Sum.

Sum was from China. She was very delicate but in comparison to Mel she hardly got noticed when the two were at the same events or parties. I asked Mel whether she could imagine what Sum must feel like, seeing all eyes on her friend and none on herself. Did she realise the impact that would have on Sum's self-confidence? Mel needed to look at her beauty not as a burden but as a blessing. She needed to be comfortable within herself and realise that not only was she blocking someone good from coming into her life, but that she was also making herself unhappy and ruining any chance of love. Wearing a radiant smile on your face does not mean you are ignorant of what's going on around you. It just means you choose to be happy instead of miserable. You let your joyful aurora shine on others. I wanted Mel to look at life differently. So far, she had been looking at it through a narrow tunnel vision, quiet, dark and straight. Yes, its true men looked at her beauty and fancied sleeping with her. They imagined what she would be like in bed and what sexual positions they could have her in. But did she give them anything different to imagine? Besides her rude, stand offish behaviour? No, she did not. She needed to let a man be a man. Men feel physical attraction first, but that didn't mean that she had to jump into bed with whoever came along. Women are quite strong mentally. They should never underestimate their powers of persuasion combined with female sexuality. The combination is almost irresistible to the opposite sex. Let a man admire your beauty, let him get interested, but influence him in a way that he discovers the real you and sees more than simply your outward beauty.

For the first time since our conversation started Mel lost her hostility towards me and started to smile, genuinely. I knew she got my point. I reminded her, if a man was handsome enough for her yet tried to attract her attention, she would get upset and remark that he had some audacity. Mel burst out laughing. We are all victims of having a certain level of hypocrisy in us. The world today is run mostly sadly on appearance.

When you go for a job interview you make sure you look your best. You make the effort to dress well, you groom yourself, and if it's a man conducting the interview then you may engage in some extra flirting. A low plunging neckline, revealing your cleavage can accessorise your natural curves. Or maybe you might undo a few extra buttons. Opposites attract and so the interviewer can't help but get distracted by the way you look.

A strong, confident individual can use their sexuality as an instrument of strength. Bait for the opposite sex and power to manipulate their partner to do their bidding.

A confident man and woman will play off each other and themselves. They will not only be good in banter together, but they will inspire each other to achieve higher goals because they are both happy and content within themselves. They'll aspire to build each other up to succeed.

On the other hand, a partner who lacks confidence will not be secure within themself and may only strive to pull the other down. As a happy partner, it can become impossible to live with someone who lacks inner worth and suffer from low self-esteem. In some cases, the unhappy partner may start to tear the other person down so that they feel superior.

Craig was 6'5"tall, dark haired, green eyed, well-built and charming. In a suit he looked like Prince Charming. He had no shortage of women throwing themselves at him. Lena was Craig's other half. She herself looked like a super model: slim and slender, 6' tall. She had waist-length, blonde hair and hazel coloured eyes. She loved Craig with all her heart, and she never minded women throwing themselves at him, simply because she knew her worth, her value and she was happy. Lena knew she turned heads, even if she wore just an ordinary pair of trousers and a t-shirt. She was simply stunning.

Since she was so confident, it didn't matter to her how many women tried throwing themselves at him if he never crossed the line, and remained faithful to her alone.

On the flip side, Craig could not handle all the attention Lena received. He was quite insecure. Not because he had any cause to be, but rather because he was not a confident person. All the confidence he portrayed outwardly was an act to protect what he lacked. Jealousy led to mistrust and soon possessiveness, which in turn led to foul language and abuse. The relationship spiralled downhill until it was not even worth labelling as a relationship. Lena, who had once loved Craig, was filled with fear, hate and regret. The relationship finally ended one day at a pub when Craig's jealousy got too much for Lena. He beat another man up because he, in Craig's view, spoke to Lena too much. He was arrested and charged with assault. Lena ended their relationship at that very moment saying, "Never look for me again, we are over. I can't take it anymore."

I remember Lena having a conversation with me a few weeks after the ordeal had taken place. She recalled how good they were together at the beginning. If only insecurity hadn't taken over for him, they might have still been together. All she wanted now was to find a man who could be her equal or else she would stay on her own for fear of

Andrea Aviet

finding another man like Craig. It's sad but it's true. If a man can't accept you for you then you need to end the relationship and vice versa. There's no point in suffocating each other.

13th July – Nymphomania revelation, sex, silk, sinful pleasure

My next friend was Amy; a gorgeous beauty from South Africa. She was stunning. At 5'9" tall, she had olive skin, hazel eyes and sandy blonde hair. She could capture anyone's attention and keep them mesmerised. Although we were all friends for quite a few years, there was something about Amy that I could never quite put my finger on. Certain behaviour she displayed never really added up with who she was. She used to make me second guess her.

Amy had a lust for lingerie, much more than the average person. We all love to buy lingerie for special occasions and for our special man. We like to wrap ourselves up in seduction. But Amy's preoccupation with lingerie was different. She would walk into a shop, feel a silk thong and sexual urges would be ignited within her. I had to dig deeper to understand her while I was on my quest. We decided to have a ladies' night out. To get away, do some crazy stuff together, just so that I could try to have a personal talk with her and get an insight into her mental state. Let me warn you, when trying to understand a complicated person, be careful what you ask for. You just might not be ready for what you're about to experience.

Andrea Aviet

Let me reveal the events of that day. We decided to go for lunch, shopping, a drink to unwind and then a massage. If time permitted, we would head down to the pub for another drink and then head home. Pretty straightforward right? No, not a chance in hell.

We met for lunch and had the healthy option of salad and some green tea. While chatting this is what I discovered: Amy had a secret. She struggled with her life and did not want to reveal her secret to anyone. However, with some persistence, she started to reveal her secret to me.

Five years ago, she was engaged and was about to get married, but on her wedding day she ended up having sex with someone else in her wedding dress. The husband caught her in the act. Wow, this left me speechless; I could not understand why on earth someone would do that on their wedding day of all days. This was beyond my understanding, way beyond. The shock I felt prevented me from responding at that moment. All I wanted to do was to curse her for being so stupid. She had a man who loved her more than life itself. And honestly, you mostly hear of women being heartbroken; the man betraying the woman, but Amy's fiancé was a wreck. It took him years to get over her; Amy was in tears as she spoke, admitting she was still in love with him. Yet, another strange remark from her, I thought. I told her she had some major issues and said she was insane. Because, in my opinion, you don't do that to someone you claim to be in love with. This was deep.

"Let's go shopping," she said.

I could hardly believe my ears.

"I'll show you something, and you'll understand," she continued.

I was quite wary about what I was supposed to get and what she was about to show me. I was not sure if I wanted to see anything after all her recent revelations...

We split the bill and left. As we walked down the busy street silently, Amy turned to me suddenly.

"Let's go in here."

It was a lingerie shop. She wanted to buy some much-needed underwear. I reminded her that she had bought some just the week before. She said it was already gone... Alarm bells went off in my head. I looked at Amy as she stroked the red satin thong. I watched her intently as she caressed the silky material. Then she began to smell the freshness of the new fabric and started to breathe a little heavily. She flicked her hair back over her shoulder while taking another deep sniff. Licking her lips, she closed her eyes and started to moan a little. It was almost as if, in some strange way, Amy started to feel sexual urges. I had to interrupt her. It was all turning a little too strange for my liking. I asked her if she was okay and that seemed to snap her out of it. She regained her composure, quickly.

"Yes, I am fine."

She smiled and said, "Let's pay up."

I began to wonder if Amy had some weird personality disorder but I thought it was not the appropriate moment to be questioning her about it.

After paying she could not wait to try her new thong on. She went straight into a public toilet to try them on and came out with the most radiant smile. That gave me a hint that she liked them. Walking down the street it was almost as if she was high on something. What I was seeing from her was unbelievable, not to mentioned awkward. We went to a bar to relax.

Amy told the bartender that she wanted a succulent, clear glass of red wine. She looked at him as if she wanted to jump on him, hold him down, straddle him and have wild sex. That's the impression she gave off. Her body language was completely changed from earlier. The bartender was cute. He would definitely have given her what she desired, but her behaviour was most inappropriate. He had a good body and was a rugged-looking man. Well Amy did not have to try too hard with men. She just had to show she was interested and they would follow the olive beauty anywhere. Amy asked this bartender when he got a break. I couldn't believe my ears. He told her he got a break at 7pm. There were only 10 minutes to go. Amy smiled and told me to wait for her, she was coming back. She walked out with him and came back at exactly 7.20pm. Part of me just wanted to get up and leave, not wait for her. But the other half wanted to dig further. I had to know what the hell was going on with her. This was out of character; it was not the Amy I knew. I really did not recognise this version of her – she certainly was not my friend, Amy. This was a stranger...

On her return she was calm, composed, not on edge. She no longer seemed to be on a high. This was the Amy I recognised and knew.

"Are you alright?"

"Yes, I am."

"Okay, tell me what's going on with you," I demanded.

She said they went to his car. She didn't want to know his name as he was one among many. She said she needed to fuck.

Andrea Aviet

I bit my tongue as I asked again, what was going on with her. I was trying not to be judgemental until I'd heard the whole story.

She looked straight into my eyes, "I did not want to, I had to. I had to fuck him, I had to fuck someone."

"Why?"

"It's the urge. I can't help myself. When it comes, it just takes over, and at that moment in time I just need someone. Any one will do. Until I fuck someone the urge keeps growing; it takes over me completely until I give in.

"Once I am done it subsides and life gets back to normal again."

Oh my God. Having been with her when the urge came on, seeing how fast the silk underwear triggered her off, was astonishing.

"Amy, this happened on your wedding day?"

"Yes", she said. "The excitement, the lace underwear I picked for my husband. I wanted to excite him on our wedding night, but I could not control myself. I came on to the other man in the heat of the moment." Tears rolled down her cheeks as she recounted the story.

She couldn't even apologise to him for what she had done. I realised that Amy was a nymphomaniac. She took risks; she experienced no pleasure while having sex. She simply had to do it, she had to perform. I wanted to know what caused this in her. What triggered it off in Amy? Was it her environment? Heredity? Life events? Or a chemical imbalance?

I began to dig a little further; Amy witnessed her mother having sex with strange men as a young girl. She witnessed the bed banging against the wall, and then when her mum caught a glimpse of her she would send her downstairs. But Amy could still hear the banging; she could hear the moans, she saw the men come down and her mother smile and wave goodbye. She saw different men every day. They came, they had sex with her mother, and then they left. They never stayed for more than a few hours. That was Amy's life. That was her earliest memories of men, relationships, sex, and it was clear that Amy never witnessed stability during her childhood. I do not have answers for what made her into the lady she was today. I understood the sad underlying issues that made her feel the need to fuck, as she put it. I understood her need to get it over with. She had witnessed this behaviour in her childhood. So now, as an adult, she tried subconsciously to justify her actions. She was now a confused woman, trying to live by burying her dark past.

Andrea Aviet

"Amy, I am so sorry." I had to say these words with deepest regret.

I asked her to be open, yet as she was sharing with me how she was trying to cope with her problem, I went from anger, to disbelief, to feeling shame, to wanting to walk out on her. I didn't want to accept the very same truth I had asked for, and by staying, it led me to witness the sadness she lived with, every day. To see how awful the entire situation was for her.

"Would you like to go for counselling?"

I told her, although others called her a slut, to me Amy would always be a friend, one who I deeply appreciated for taking me on the journey of discovering what lay behind her actions.

That was so brave of her to let me see her for who she really was. How many of us can open up like that? It's not easy. We all wear masks and hide who we are. The mask we wear protects us from who we really are. It covers the flaws, hides imperfections, manipulates, disguises and alters our character, so we display ourselves through the narrow pre-approved vision which others have of us. We are all guilty of wearing a mask. Many of us have baggage; a past which has not been resolved entirely. We carry that residue within us. We carry so many different burdens, it would be perfect to just let go of them all. To let that heaviness be left behind somewhere in the abyss of time and start afresh.

I believe in new beginnings. At any given point in time, anyone can take their destiny into their own hands and start fresh. It just depends on a person's mindset. Are you willing to fight for what you believe in? What kind of life do you want to lead? One of a loose cannon or one of absolute control? I believe Amy had the inner strength to change her life around. Until now she just did not believe she could. She felt that her secret was so dark, so horrific, that no one would accept nor understand her. Yet when she revealed it to me and what she had lived with, in a way it set her free. The fear of being judged imprisoned her. Amy, unknowingly, managed to set herself free, I felt.

I headed back home. I needed some sleep in preparation for the long, tiring day I had to look forward to, tomorrow. How many of us hate Mondays? The hangover, loads of work to catch up on because the weekend got in the way and things just piled up. Well I could not wait to get into a nice hot bubble bath, play some soft music and just relax. Later, I would sink into my kingsize, comfortable bed where dreams would come to me in the silence of a peaceful night. I had an hour-long journey travelling back to London, over ground, underground... Although I was exhausted the crowds kept me alert until I got home.

Andrea Aviet

18ᵗʰ July – Love scenes

I noticed some elderly couples who were travelling together. One couple in particular came to my attention. They were laughing, enjoying each other's company. I noticed how her little delicate arm was placed through his. As they sat together quietly, the noise from the rest of the compartment did not seem to bother them. It was as if they were both lost in a little bubble which surrounded them. Radiance and joy emitted from them. Their eyes twinkled as they spoke to each other. Wow, I thought, how beautiful it is to see that.

Their faces were aged, their skin was lined and wrinkled with maturity, experience and history. I wondered is this was new acquaintance, or a love grown and blossomed over the years. There was a purity there. A caring nature which looked as if it had been nurtured over time. Besides the attraction of true inner beauty there was nothing else. No random sudden sex craves, nothing to resemble the behaviour of a youthful couple. They made me smile. Who knows what their story was? But if it had been quieter on the train, I would definitely have ventured over to them to find out more about them. But the timing did not seem appropriate and, amongst the noise, I would not have got an accurate narration from them.

Andrea Aviet

On the opposite side of the train, a few rows ahead of me, sat a young teenage couple. The young lad had piercings along his brow, a stud on his tongue and a little ring on his lip. His girlfriend was the same. While he wore trousers and a shirt she had the shortest of skirts, fish net stockings and purple hair. Both chewed gum, spoke in loud, unrefined voices and blasted music from one of their smartphones. They spoke so loudly that even if you didn't want to hear the conversation you had no choice. Common friends, parties, drugs, drinking, group sex, watching pornography were all the hot topics being discussed between the two. They were going to a party which promised to deliver all of the above. The girlfriend was telling him that he could not agree to or enter into any sexual group activities if she was not there with him. He laughed and slid his hand up her slim thighs. He rested his hand on her leg as he started to kiss her in the crowded compartment. It didn't matter to them who was around, or what anyone heard.

"What you looking at? You never seen anyone in love before?" they shouted at anyone they caught looking at them.

What a difference in values and relationships, displayed between the two couples. The young lad professed to be in love. No way was he in love. He was just young and mistaken. He had much to learn and hopefully time would teach them both right from wrong.

There were so many things happening on this train. There was a woman sitting by herself playing with her wedding ring. She turned it round and around her finger. She was lost in a deep, troubled thought. She gripped her phone tightly as if she was clinging on to it for dear life. Perhaps its very presence was giving her support in some way. Was she waiting eagerly to receive a call or to make one?

A young professional couple stood near the door. Both were well-dressed in suits. As the young lady stood close and rested her head on the gentleman's shoulder, he smiled, stroked her hair and spoke gently to her.

"Not long to go honey, you're tired. We'll be home soon." He placed a gentle kiss on her cheek.

A few metres away, a pleasant-looking young lady was sitting in one of the seats. Her whole attention was pinned on the professional couple. She looked as if she wanted to be a part of what they had. Maybe she longed for a relationship?

A few business men sat reading their newspapers. One got a call and started discussing what he would like for dinner. He ended the conversation with, "I love you and can't wait to see you".

Andrea Aviet

When I got to my stop, I jumped off the train quickly, glad to be almost home.

As soon as I walked through my front door, I put the kettle on to make a cup of coffee and ran myself a bath. I put on some soft music in the background. As I soaked and relaxed in my herbal bubble bath, the tension and stress left my body. It helped me unwind and get ready to tuck myself into bed.

18ᵗʰ July – Dreams do come true (cont)

As I lay my head gently on my pillow and pulled my soft quilt over me, the music still played in the background. It was difficult not to recall the events of the day. I thought about Amy and wished her only the best. I tried to make a mental note of the day's agenda for Monday.

Sedrick, an Italian friend of mine, had always displayed a keen interest in me. It seemed he'd decided to surprise me.

Not only did we work together, but he was also my boss. That made the situation awkward. I knew he had a silent interest in me. One day, he informed me that I did not need to work today and that he had some other plans in store for us. I had a huge pile of work on my desk but Sedrick insisted on not wanting to argue, so I obliged. We left the office together. He said he wanted to show me something. So, we went for lunch and he started a conversation which I thought was rather personal. He wanted to find out why I was single? Why did I not date anyone? The lunch was an excellent compensation for such personal questions so I answered them willingly. Sedrick ordered a bottle of wine, which relaxed us and lightened our spirits. I started to enjoy his company and, although I had tried to avoid looking at him in the past, especially when he smiled, that was proving more difficult when we were sat at a table, alone. Now, every time he smiled, I got more drawn towards him. We noticed each other for the first time and really made note of each other's actions.

I find it strange that you can be with someone, see them day in and day out, but not actually notice them. Time passed by and it was time to go home. Sedrick offered to walk me home. When we got to my house, he kissed me. I wished we had all day. I looked into his eyes, saw his smile. He raised his hand to hold me steady while again he kissed me once more. I didn't try to stop him. I didn't want to. My smile, followed by laughter, gave him the long-awaited consent which he had been eagerly on the lookout for. I unlocked my front door and turned to usher Sedrick in. That's when he scooped me up and carried me through the door. He shut the door behind us with his hip.

"I've been waiting for this moment for a very long time."

I liked the way he lifted me up with such ease. I liked the way he held me close and the gentle way he put me down on the bed, tripping over me. I laughed at his clumsiness. He seemed to be in awe of me. His look of passion was indescribable. The way he kissed my neck sent shivers right down by spine. Moonlight filtered through the lace curtain at my bedroom window. In the soft light he looked so appealing. Was this attraction? Was it lust? Was it loneliness? I didn't know how to categorise it. But every curve on his body looked enhanced, irresistible. My body craved him, longed for his touch. Desire ruled my every sensation until Sedrick finally penetrated me. As he did he held me tight, saying he was in love with me.

My eyes opened in shock. An awful noise escaped my lips. But I was in bed alone.

"Sedrick?"

There was no reply. The music still played softly in the background, and I was still lying in bed with my satin red nightgown on. It had been a dream; it took a few moments for me to get back into reality. Oh dear, how was I supposed to pull myself out of what seemed so real?

Time was not being kind to me. It was Monday morning and I started to get myself together and rush off to work. I got to work 10 minutes late, oh no.

Sedrick was stood right in front of the door the office, blocking my way. He turned to me as I approached and told me we were late for a presentation. Luckily, the other party had not arrived yet, which bought me some time.

Andrea Aviet

Under pressure, Sedrick would try to undermine his staff. I decided to front up to him. I stood close, looked him straight in the eyes, smiled and tossed my hair. The look I gave him said 'Really? You want me to go there?' He was taken aback. This had never happened to him before; no one ever did that to him. The moment quickly passed and the meeting went ahead. The presentation was a success and both sides were happy. My colleague Ted asked me if I was feeling alright and what was that all about with me and the boss? I started to laugh out loud.

"I had a bad dream last night, but it's nothing." I hadn't realised anyone had seen me confront Sedrick. It wasn't only Ted that had noticed, but others too. They described my actions as bold, radiant and playful. They just left me blushing. A few hours later Sedrick called me in to his room and asked me to have lunch with him. I really don't know what came over me but I questioned him. Was he asking me out? If indeed he was, I didn't think lunch in his office was a very appealing invitation. I wanted him to know I was not easy, that I had standards and if he wanted my company, I was neither easy nor cheap. No work lunchtime meal was going to sweep me off my feet. He smiled.

"I asked you to join me for lunch, I did not say where. I am still waiting for an answer."

Opaque Desires

"Yes, I will join you for lunch,"

We left the office together, and he drove me to the most gorgeous restaurant.

Over lunch, we talked about things in general. I didn't know what the future had planned for us, but a seed had been sowed. Would my dream become a reality in the near future?

Andrea Aviet

19ᵗʰ July – The envious eye

While sitting at my cubical, the conversation between a few workmates got my attention. They were talking about someone in particular. About how negative she was, how her attitude was disgusting, that she slandered everyone. She would talk so sweetly in front of a person, but as soon as their back was turned she would slander the very same person to anyone who would listen. The name of this person was never mentioned. They were quite careful in that regard.

Even so, we all knew who they were talking about. There was only one bitterly negative lady in the office. She was like a rotten apple trying to rot everyone around her.

Gena had a good job at our company. She was married with children. She'd had the big white wedding which most women dream of, the big white house, a husband and a ring on her finger. He earned very well, so money was no issue. So why was it that this woman, who had everything most women would kill for, just envied what everyone else had? What an irony.

Something did not seem right about Gena. She didn't resonate well within my spirit. There was truly a lot more than met the eye, under the surface.

Have you ever noticed that if you feel you're overweight, immediately you assume others are overweight too? You start to be negative, criticize them, find flaws and that actually portrays your inner self. The way you actually see yourself. Most people don't realise when they start to tear others down, it's they themselves who lack confidence. By putting someone down it makes them feel good about themself. Either that, or they desire what the other person has; jealousy dictates their every action till it keeps eating away at their soul. Either they try to tear someone's appearance down, bring back and highlight any error from their past they are aware of, or simply question every action of theirs because they dislike the person because they have something which they envy. How fast are we to judge another without hesitation? Without even stopping to think we too have a history?

I started to look closely at her. I observed her speech, and paid attention when she spoke about her personal life. It was undeniable that the lady was seriously unhappy. The wonderful big white wedding dream had been a reality for her, but she also had the coldness of the white wedding too. Her husband put the ring on her finger but she worked alone for the family, for the children. There was no partnership, just a dictatorship. One partner did everything, while the other did nothing.

Gina and her husband had their children before they married. She knew what he was like but instead of choosing to end their relationship, she decided to let fear rule her and walk down the aisle. For better or for worse, till death do us apart.

She envied the life of a single woman. She even envied the life of a single mother. They were much braver than she would ever be. They managed on their own. Even when problems crossed their path, they were driven by determination and the will to succeed. They only had themselves to rely on, with no one by their side. Gena thought about her car, her huge house and the mortgage that came with it. She would never manage on her own. She often grumbled about how she had to pick up after her husband. How, instead of having three children, it was like having four. He never thought about her on special occasions. Mother's Day, birthdays, Valentine's Day, all passed by without any effort.

But she alone could make changes in her life; she chose the big house, the car, the pretence. And with it came coldness, loneliness. Gina tried very hard to work on her relationship, but you can't clap with one hand. Similarly, for a relationship to work both parties have to try. Sometimes you need to know when to stay and when to simply walk away.

Marriage is a partnership. It's two people coming together to join their lives, finances, likes and dislikes, dreams and aspirations. If one falls, the other picks up and supports. It's not to work separately, but as a team. A union where dreams are nurtured and family values instilled, while being built together.

The road to happiness seldom comes easily, otherwise we would all have it and never appreciate it. Difficulty makes the road to joy a lot more meaningful and appreciated.

There was a reason why I was single at this point in my life. Many mistakes made in haste. Wrong men and paths taken in the quest of finding love. I'd been led by youthful impatience rather than mature wisdom. I wanted to find the right man. Not one who would want to rule over me but someone who could accept me for me. I have not found him yet, the man who would excite me, understand my needs sexually, mentally and emotionally. A man who would let me in and be an equal partner. One who would share his ambitions with me. Allow me to partake of his ambition, his desires. In return he would respect my drive and my ambitions. My special love would be unique. He would bond, truly, with my soul. Until I find him I'll never settle, because settling would just be undermining my own value and cheating myself out of true happiness. I know I will find him some day. Don't ask me when, I don't know. The answers lie among the elements of fate, destiny and direction from up above.

But in the quietness of the still night, when I go for a long walk under a blanket of stars, I sometimes feel a gush of wind come my way. I speak to the spirits of the night and ask them to carry my essence to my soulmate. If he is out there, let him feel my energy in his spirit. Let him see me from afar in his mind's eye and let the stars light up his path so that he can follow my trail and join me under the moonlight where warmth, love, unity and joy can bind our two hearts together. Maybe, this is the hopeless romantic I have let unleashed and shared with you.

But who says it's not good to dream. I find that fortune favours the bold and those who dare to dream realistically, bear beautiful fruits, exquisitely developed to one's own taste and desire.

20ᵗʰ July – Double identity, confessions of a prostitute

While I continued to walk along enjoying the peaceful, quiet night, I felt a little thirsty. I turned onto a street that was new to me. It bustled with people, all going about their business on this lovely evening. I tried to find a newsagent, at which I could buy a drink. At first that's all I focused on, until I recognised a familiar face. What perfect timing. And a lovely coincidence too. Hoping she would know the area I decided to cross over to where she stood. At first the high street was quite busy and the number of cars passing on the two-way street proved to be quite a challenge to cross. Eventually I managed to cross and made it over to Kim.

"Oh, I must say it's great to see you here! Can you help me find Oscar Road please, I think I am lost."

That's the question I put across with a friendly smile.

Kim and I pass each other every morning and every night. Even when we're in a hurry, we always acknowledge each other and say hi. But today, I got the most bizarre reaction from Kim.

"I am sorry, you mistake me for someone else, please leave me alone." She looked straight into my

151

eyes as she said the words. I looked the same as I always did. There was no change there, yet there was a complete transformation in her.

Her hair was styled in waves, which seemed to have a life of its own, tossing and dancing in the wind. She wore beautiful makeup; her eyes were enhanced and well-defined by her mascara and eye liner. It drew attention to her blue eyes. The blush was perfect, lips as red as fresh, ripe strawberries. The fishnet stockings she wore looked beautiful with her short figure-hugging, red dress which seemed to accentuate her long, slender legs. She didn't move from the spot. Who was she waiting for? Perhaps she was trying to get rid of me because she was waiting for her partner?

I spotted a little corner shop and headed inside to buy some water. When I came out again, having asked the shopkeeper for directions, there was a white Mercedes parked on the street in front of Kim. She spoke to someone in the car. He extended his hand to her; she shook it and got in. Our eyes met briefly as she climbed into the car. My instant reaction was to wave goodbye. Kim looked tempted to do the same. But instead she did nothing and was driven away down the long, busy road, somewhere into the night. I don't know why but I just couldn't get our meeting out of my head.

Common sense prickled me. In a normal situation you don't refuse to acknowledge people, or ignore people you recognise, if you're going on a date. Unless you don't want to be recognised. When would our paths cross again?

A few days passed and there was no sign of her. Should I be worried about her? Another week went by so I decided to retrace my step from that night in the hope of meeting up with Kim again.

I waited on the bustling street, and sure enough, at 9pm she seemed to appear from out of nowhere. Where did she come from? She did exactly what she had earlier in the week. She stood in the exact same place but this time a different car approached. The driver stopped, they shook hands and she got in again. No, it could not be? I must be wrong, she could not be?

Could Kim be into prostitution? It had nothing to do with me, yet given my present quest, I felt the need to try and approach her. Prostitution and Kim? It didn't make sense. She just didn't seem the type. Well, I went back the next day and waited for her to show up. She never did. A week passed and there was no sign of her.

On the 18th day since I last saw her being driven away, she once again reappeared on the same street.

Andrea Aviet

"Hey, Kim!" I called out across the street. "We need to talk."

She turned and walked away quickly.

"Please stop" I called out, "I'll pay you."

Kim stopped dead in her tracks. She turned to me, then.

"I beg your pardon? What did you say?"

"I'll pay you, just stop, please"

The embarrassment and confusion on her face was crystal clear.

"You know what I do?"

"Yes, I kind of, figured it out. Let's go for a coffee?"

She could not believe that, knowing who she was and what she did, I still wanted to have coffee with her. Be seen in public with her.

"Are you sure?"

I smiled. "Yes, of course."

We walked down to the nearest pub; I was desperate for a coffee. All of the waiting around for Kim had tired me out. At first Kim was quite defensive, apprehensive and worried about why I had such an interest in her. To be fair, if someone was so interested in me, I too would be sceptical. Breaking the ice with her was no easy task.

We both wanted to find out each other's motives. I wanted to understand her, because the subject of sex and prostitution deeply fascinated me. Why do women go down that route? Do they not feel any attachment on any level for the multiply partners they sleep with? Do they use protection? Do they fear sexually transmitted diseases? I could think of a million questions.

However, Kim's interest lay in finding out what my motives were and did I want to try to ruin her business?

"Kim, I really don't want anything else from you except information, guidance and insight from you, regarding your world," I explained, carefully. "There's no interest from my side to join your trade or to spoil your business in any way. My only interest is in understanding your profession."

The expression on her face was one of disbelief, shock and confusion.

She remarked that she had lost all of her friends once they discovered what she did in her spare time. She was in awe of my description of prostitution (although she found it difficult to name it out loud). I talked about it with respect and without condemnation.

Well, I always had the ability to see things differently. It stemmed from my youthful days.

My analysis in regard to any profession was, skills are perfected over time and developed. No skill is developed overnight. Rather it evolves, perfects and helps you reach a level of financial stability and. You turn up at a certain time, you work during that time frame, satisfy your clients, deliver the highest standard of customer service to ensure you have both a loyal and continuing client base. Whatever the profession, the necessary basics are the same.

A skill where monetary transactions pass hands between seller and buyer. Is this not the basis of every profession? Skill development, working environment, transactions and expansion of customer data, networking.

Although I am not condoning and praising the profession of prostitution, I do understand that many women use their sexuality and treat it as a profession in the game of survival and earning a livelihood. If one enters voluntarily into it, then noone should condemn them. All of us have freedom of choice, to choose who we want to be.

After hearing my ideological beliefs, Kim felt more relaxed and happy that someone out there did not judge her actions, but rather respected her as a person. We sat exchanging views and spoke for hours. She was so relaxed that she ordered dinner for us both, on her tab.

We relaxed together and spent time. Much later Kim started to open up to me. "What's it like?"

"Well it's like any other job. Either you like what you do or you just hate it and never go back to it. But like most people, if you have bills to pay and need to work, you do whatever it takes to get by."

"Is it easy to have sex with strangers?"

"Well, yes and no. If you get a nice client, a rich, posh, well-educated man who just wants a woman to show him a good time, he'll treat you well. He might buy you gifts depending on how good you are at satisfying his every need. Some men are so busy that they just need a woman when they have the time for one. But in an ideal world, we women want men to give us time every day, give us attention and make us their priority. The men who come to me don't have the time for that. They have work stress and commitments, so when they want to relax, they need someone who is willing to offer casual sex, on call companionship without commitments. In return I'm compensated with financial gain. Sometimes, you might get some men who are a little weird, some aggressive and others have unreasonable demands.

"Others might want to record the entire sexual encounter; I am not comfortable with that demand and so I refuse. Some like to hit I am against that too," Kim explained.

"I can't handle rough sex and violence."

When Kim books on to a job, or before accepting a self-chosen assignment, she usually sends out a private agreement form to new clients, informing them upfront of the dos and don'ts of the service she provides. If, for any reason, there is any violation of terms of agreement she refuses to deal with them in the future and might even sue them for any inappropriate behaviour.

Wow. Kim had both my attention and admiration. She had such a well thought-through approach and had taken steps to ensure her own personal safety.

"Do you have sex with married men or just single men?"

"Well, any man who treats me well. Most of these men have wives who are so taken up with their rich lifestyle. Most of them even have their toy boys on the side. While the husbands are away the wives are at play. Of course, it's not that way with all rich wives, but a few who I have come to have personal dealings with. Some husbands just want to have some role play with their wife, but she may not be willing to oblige.

"I had one client who wanted his wife to dress up as a sexy secretary. He asked her to pretend to be bending over, cleaning his table. But he wanted her to wear a thong and a skirt which was just covering her behind. A white, transparent long-sleeved shirt without a bra, so he could see her nipples, and he could get an erection easily. He told me he wanted to tear her thong off with his teeth, lick her, give her oral sex and then bend her over the table. He wanted to fuck her hard from behind until he came. But his wife, although she was 20 years younger and looked like a super model, would not oblige his sexual fantasy."

Up until now, I was the one asking questions. But all of a sudden Kim turned to me with a question.

"What are your thoughts about a married couple's relationship where the wife doesn't want to please her husband? Do you think I am wrong for being the other woman, although it means nothing to me?"

I wasn't expecting to be questioned and was taken off guard. But in all fairness, if you're asking someone personal questions at such an intimate level, I guess I should have been prepared to answer some as well.

After thinking about it for a while, I replied "I think it's important to remember that marriage is a union, along with a promise of commitment to love each other, unconditionally. So, if a husband wants to have sex with his wife, spice up their relationship, try new things, it's not a negative thing. As long as it leaves them both satisfied, why not?

"Of course, the wife should be up for it and partake. As long as he does not abuse their bond, disrespect her or try to physically harm her in a way with force and violence. Men and women can change over time. Interest in sex diminishes. Yet I feel sex and intimacy play an important part in maintaining a healthy relationship. So why are couples not taking the time and hearing what their partner desires?"

I don't necessary condone what Kim was doing. But in today's world, if it's not Kim it would just be someone else. I understood, for her, it was a business transaction, but would the client's wife care? Was she herself getting satisfaction elsewhere?

Who knows. The answers to certain questions are not as straight forward as one might think them to be. If a partner makes a request to you to fulfil a need and you're not willing to do so, you are not taking into consideration what the other wants. So how does your relationship survive? That's the most important question to ask. You are giving the other partner an opportunity to look elsewhere. Yes, people should be faithful. But in my opinion, if my other half asks me for something, I am going to be quite open to it, as long as it's within reason. Simply because I'll be happy that he's approaching me and being upfront regarding what he needs from me.

Many a time it's hard for men to open up about his unmet desires if he really loves his partner. No matter how much love there is, he will start to stray away. I say this because if love exists between two people, so should compromise. That's what makes a couple stay together, happily.

What are you giving your man to love at the end of the day? If you're not giving him something, where does he turn? Some love their woman too much to walk away, but go elsewhere to get sexual fulfilment because they have accepted that their own partners will not be willing to satisfy their desires.

I don't condone infidelity, yet we need to ask why does one go down that route? What causes it? Sometimes a partner may be very faithful, loving and simply perfect, yet the other might end up cheating. It's just lack of self-control and a great deal of foolishness.

Andrea Aviet

3rd August – Man stripped of love

Sometimes people don't value what they have, or respect it, until it's too late and lost forever. I remember a colleague from a few years ago who had an awful experience. He was a very faithful gentleman, true to the meaning of the word. It was so upsetting to find out that his partner was having an affair.

As soon as the husband would leave for work, the wife would summon their neighbour to her bedroom. How she did it, I don't know. Did she love her partner?

One day, Derek came home early. It was their wedding anniversary so he was brandishing a beautiful bunch of flowers, a box of luxurious chocolates and a little gift bag. He came rushing in, beaming with joy, ready to spoil his wife on their special day. Jillian had no clue he was returning home early. She was too caught up with the young, well-built gardener, who just happened to be their neighbour.

Derek went upstairs looking for his wife, when he found the ground floor of the house deserted. A few minutes later, neighbours heard a commotion coming from one of the bedrooms; lots of shouting and screaming. Normally their household was a very quiet one. Today, however, was a day no one on Grace Street would ever forget. Furniture came flying out of the window. The shouting and screaming carried on.

"Oh my God! I am sorry, I am so sorry. You weren't supposed to be back."

Then everyone saw Derek drag Jillian out of the house. She was wrapped in a bed sheet and had tears streaming down her face. The pair were quickly followed by the pretty boy neighbour whose face was blotched with red marks. As was Derek's. He threw Jillian and all of her belongings onto the street. He told her if she didn't remove it quickly, he would set a light to it all.

There's a limit. A very fine line in a relationship, between taking advantage of someone's good nature and love and walking all over them because you think they are passive.

Jillian had pushed Derek too far. He was hurting; he trusted her, provided and did everything she ever asked.

What did that pretty boy have over him? Derek was frantic, demanding to know. Sadly, Jillian's lust had been driven by physical impulse. His smell, the way he sweated while doing the gardening, the way he took his shirt off to reveal his bare chest under the hot sun. All these things together had triggered her sexual desires. She longed for him. Her body craved his touch and when she was with him, she felt younger, alive and excited.

Derek was heartbroken.

"Does he love, you like I do?"

Jillian could not answer. She stared at him silently. Derek was broken, his heart shattered into a million pieces. He broke down and wept.

"I gave you everything!" he shouted. "I did whatever you wanted. All you had to do was ask. And this is how you return my love? You have broken my trust and our marriage. How could you do this to us, how?"

Although Jillian pleaded for his forgiveness, she had made her bed now she had to lie in it. She had lost true love just because of craving desires of the flesh. Looks don't last. The gardener's fit body will not be forever firm, smooth and wrinkle free. But true love is constant and forever. It never ages, never fades and never loses its beauty. On the contrary, in time its beauty is enhanced.

"You destroyed us. We are over. Just walk away."

That was the end. From that day the man we knew was gone forever. He began seeing prostitutes like Kim. He would change the women he saw on a regular basis. Sometimes he would be seeing multiple women at a time. The man had changed completely.

He was no longer loving, respecting, and caring. The hurt, the betrayal he had felt at the hand of his wife had turned him into a man without a soul. All he did was satisfy his need for sex. Every time he needed it he called upon a call girl, visited a brothel or picked up a prostitute. Call it what you like, his feelings, love, emotion, they all ceased to exist to him. One woman's mistake changed a true, devoted man into a rotten shell.

Derek couldn't mend his broken heart. Nor could he let anyone close to him ever again. Needs must be met so he did whatever he had to.

One always has to look at actions, reactions, causes and outcomes. It's never possible to condemn someone based upon just what you see them doing at one particular point in time.

I continued to question Kim.

"Do you use protection?"

Kim went on to tell me she would not take birth control pills and was against all sorts of condoms. Female condoms in particular were a big turn off for her. She described it as spoiling her sex drive. Of course I wanted to find out why. She explained that they are a lot bigger than male condoms.

"If you meet a client and you are both up and ready for an erotic night, taking the time to put in a female condom spoils the moment. Having to navigate the man's penis past the ring, into the condom so that it doesn't miss the target area and go straight into your vagina, is yet another problem. When a man's ready, he's just ready," she explained.

"It does protect against STDs and unwanted pregnancies, however it's just not for me."

Neither did Kim like men wearing condoms. She said if one of her clients did insist she would just have to fake an orgasm. Besides, she dealt with high profile clients. Most of them, she explained, get checked for STDs on a regular basis. She would also get private health checks done on herself on a regular basis. She preferred to have the implant to prevent unwanted pregnancies.

As for getting attached emotionally and developing feelings, that was a tricky one. When you learn a new trade, you have to make many a mistake until you master your skills. Then you can become not only a professional but a perfectionist. She had learned, through heart break, that she would always be the other woman in all these men's lives.

She could provide for them, fulfil a missing need which their own wives and partners could not fulfil. But experience had taught her the bitter truth that if she allowed herself to have feelings, she would be broken again. So, the only option for her was to harden her heart, making sure she would not get hurt ever again. She had to concentrate on keeping her profession down to business transactions only. Kim was the best in her field, meaning she was able to command whatever price she liked for her outstanding service without any strings attached. She had no personal lover.

I wanted to know more about her. She was most interesting.

5ᵗʰ August – The big reveal

Finally, when we met up again I decided to ask Kim how she had become a prostitute.

What lay behind this beautiful sensation wanting to do this for a living? She was clearly intelligent, so why choose this path? What provoked this choice?

On questioning her, she hesitated. She looked at me silently for a few moments, then remarked "I don't know what it is about you, but I want to open up. It would be nice to share with someone why I do this."

While Kim was at university, her mum had become widowed. She was unable to run her husband's business, and instead trusted so called friends to run it on her behalf. These 'friends' ran the business into the ground, leaving Kim's Mum with no form of income. All of a sudden Kim found that life as she knew it had changed forever. Her father had passed, and now her mother's health was deteriorating. The family business was lost and their house was repossessed. Her world was falling apart. Though her mum was sick, she worked harder than ever to support Kim's university expenses and struggled to making ends meet.

Kim took on a waitressing job at a local bar to pay bills and support her mother.

On one dark, stormy night, Kim cleaned put everything in place ready for the next day. She was exhausted and decided to take a different route home. One which would get her home a lot quicker. She walked down to the new bus stop, cutting 10 minutes off her usual route. A car drove passed and slowed down next to her. She could see some boys she had served earlier in the bar. They shouted out and asked if she wanted a lift. She declined and they passed her saying goodnight. Ten minutes later the bus finally came. When she got home she found her mother on the floor. She had collapsed through exhaustion and ill health. Kim knew her mother no longer could work, slaving to make ends meet. Her mother's only wish, no matter what happened in life, was to see Kim graduate.

That semester there was a party. Kim had fallen victim to the date rape drug. All she remembered was waking up on a bed, naked, with £10 and £20 notes flung all over her body. Sadly, proving what she supposed had happened, was close to impossible.

She had no idea who had done this to her, and no way of finding out. Instead she picked up all the money, found her clothes and walked out of the strange house that reeked of alcohol. From that day Kim went into the field of prostitution to fulfil the promise of finishing her university to her mother. She paid the bills, looked after her mother's medical expenses and could afford to stay on to finish her course. What more can one ask from a loving daughter?

I sat in shock. Her experience might have broken a lesser woman. But it had simply made Kim stronger. She had not let it destroy her. Sadly, she lost her self-worth. It had affected Kim, but I would definitely say it did not break her. In many universities, date rape drugs such as XTC, Rohypnol and Ketamine, are used on a regular basis. Youngsters need to be careful, as Kim pointed out to me.

The reasons that lay behind her path were breathtaking. She had been raped but had showed incredible strength of character, not only for herself, but also her feeble mother. Her education was not enough to secure the job she required in order to pay the bills. Being a new graduate without any work experience made it even harder. Thus, this was the only way she coped with her past. Most fascinating.

Kim's friends simply saw a prostitute when they looked at her. Someone who was much lower than them, unworthy of their friendship. I saw a loving daughter trying her best and giving her all. A strong woman and a survivor. From the bottom of my heart I thanked her for shedding insight upon her life. She taught me a valuable lesson: never judge someone based on appearance and never look down on someone else's life. For what made them arrive at their destination, the journey they had to undergo, you will never know by just looking at them externally. In order to know a person, you really have to dig deep beneath all the superficiality and uncover their true nature. Many of us are guilty of questioning why people do what they do, yet how many of us can live the life that person lives? No two people can walk down the same road.

We parted ways but my thoughts were still on Kim. This was a beautiful start to a new, open, frank friendship. It's an absolute delight when you can be yourself and take comfort in knowing there's no fear of being judged.

Andrea Aviet

6th August – Erotic group sex, lesbians, bisexuals

I had been given insightful, priceless information. Now it was time for me to get myself together and get back home. I needed to catch up on some much-needed rest, for yet another day at work awaited me tomorrow.

While I searched in my beautiful, red handbag for my house keys, my mobile rang. I looked at the time: 11.30 pm. I didn't really want to answer the phone at that time of night, so I ignored it, let myself in and headed for bed. But the caller was persistent. Just before midnight I relented and answered my phone. I knew there could be nothing positive to come of any conversation at this time of night.

When I put the phone to my ear, all I heard was "Fucking hell!" There was shouting and screaming in the background and my friend Mandy's voice pleaded. "You've got to come to my place, please."

"Oh no! What's up?" I badly needed to sleep.

Mandy was having a meltdown.

"Please come and get me, please. I am begging you"

She texted the address to me; I was fuming but I left to fetch her. My taxi pulled up in front of a huge house. I looked for Mandy while the taxi waited for us. I spotted her by the pool where she sat, completely naked.

"What happened? Where are your clothes?" I knew Mandy dating a bisexual partner.

Let me recap quickly.

Mandy and her partner would go everywhere. Joy was attracted to both men and women, depending on her sexual need at any given moment. Mandy was a lesbian. Mandy had been prepared for an exotic night with Joy, but her plans had fallen apart. They broke like shattered glass. She was in no way prepared for the shock, the devastation she was going to face that night.

Mandy had knocked on Joy's door dressed in a black, transparent body stocking with a long black whip, black stilettos and a black dildo. She had been all ready for play time. She wanted to make it special and even invited two more women. It was going to be the couple's first ever foursome. She had planned a wild sex night, full of woman, ass, nipples, sex toys, games and more fun. Poles, handcuffs, sturdy chairs, pornographic movies and drinks. It was to be a night of orgasms, screams and shrieks of pleasure. Mandy had done lots of planning. Sex tapes, a videographer and lubrications had all been paid for upfront. It had all arrived, but when Mandy walked in she was extremely upset. She found the playmates, clad in leather-look police uniforms, had already started the party. They were wearing thongs and had their legs wrapped around a pole, the dildos were already strapped on and the games had begun without her. Even more mind blowing, from a foursome it had turned into a fully-fledged gang bang sex room. Partners were switching and swapping, there were some multiple partnerships happening, there were men and women there. Mandy felt sick to her stomach.

"This was supposed to be our night. How could you do this? *Why* would you do this?" Mandy yelled at Joy. "I planned the perfect night for us."#

Joy tried her best to calm Mandy down. She apologised. She tried to get her lover undressed, she kissed her. She pushed Mandy up against the fridge door, took out a black tea towel and tied her hands gently to the handles. Then she parted her legs and, while she fingered her, she sucked on her tender breast. She sucked hard. Harder and harder. Mandy moaned. It hurt her but it felt good. She wanted more. Joy got strapped up and went down on all fours. She licked wildly between her legs, around her clitoris. Mandy was in heaven. But then Joy got so turned on that she became distracted by a passing man and started to give him a blowjob. Mandy stood helpless as Joy walked off to join the rest of the playmates, leaving her tethered to the fridge. Before long, Joy started doing a 69 with the same guy.

"Really?" Mandy shouted over to Joy. "After I went to all the trouble of planning this night, you leave me here?"

Mandy finished telling me how the night had ended...

"I organised it all and she has broken my trust.

She looked up from her seat next to the pool. She looked miserable, defeated.

"Say something!" She yelled at me.

So, I told Mandy she needed to find some clothes and leave.

"Let's get out of here, it's very late."

In a few hours it would be time to go to work and this was neither the time nor the place to be discussing this matter.

Andrea Aviet

The clock struck 1am and still there was no sign of her moving. I found some clothes and called another taxi to take us home. Convincing her to leave was yet another ordeal as she wanted her partner to leave too. I could clearly see there was no chance of that happening. We finally got out and into the cab but I knew there was no way I would be able to go to work the next day. I resigned myself to the fact that I would have to call in sick instead. Although I was annoyed and exhausted, it was evident that it was going to be a very long night. We got back to my place and I put the kettle on. I needed caffeine to keep me away. This had turned out to be a very long day.

Making coffee and setting up the spare bed for her was the least I could do.

"What do I do?" she asked. "I love her."

But I was confused myself. This situation was new to me, what could be said? This was not something I really wanted to comment on. This was someone else's relationship, their perspective on their intimacy. I decided it was much better not to comment rather than make presumptions when it comes to someone else's life.

So politely, I tried to steer her to give her outlook on the relationship as a whole, not necessarily based on tonight. I knew that, based on tonight, there would be disappointment, anger, betrayal and a loss of faith in her partner. What I aimed to discover was what the entire relationship was like. Mandy needed a whisky to calm her nerves and I needed a coffee to stay awake.

She felt the need to recap their entire relationship and I battled to stay awake. I was desperately in need of desperate sleep, it was nearing 3am.

"Are you listening to me?"

I had dozed off. Had I been speaking to her in my sleep? I had no idea.

"I was talking about our sex life." That got my attention and chased the sleep out of me.

My curiosity was aroused. I didn't know much about lesbian sex so I was interested to hear about it.

Mandy asked me if I had ever been so sexually satisfied that I wanted to be with that one exclusive partner who respected me and satisfied me beyond my wildest imagination?

Besides Edward, who satisfied my every need, who made passionate love to me because he loved the art of love making, no one else came close. She brought his memory back from the deepest part of my subconscious. It is true that sometime in your life there will be one special person who will do everything to make their mark on you. That's a special moment and if they are really good, no one else will be able to match up. They imprint on you forever. Yes, I know too well what Mandy spoke of.

"Have you ever experienced true pleasure?" she asked.

I didn't want to talk about Edward. So, Mandy told me about Joy. She told me what a perfectionist she was. How she pushed every limit and just when she thought she could not get better, she exceeded her expectations. Sex was never a problem, excitement never ceased. I gave Mandy my undivided attention. It was great to be finally learning about relationships between same sex partners.

Mandy had first met her partner when Joy worked behind a bar. She mixed drinks skilfully and had a vibe about her that grabbed Mandy's attention. There was an instant attraction. She couldn't quite put her finger on it, but they struck up a conversation, exchanged numbers, smiles and had a good laugh sitting at the bar. There were others too, but there was chemistry between the two of them.

"When there's common interest and signals you just know," Mandy explained. "You feel it and then you get butterflies in your stomach, you sigh, you blush and you know you're interested in each other.

We hung around at the bar a lot. Finally, one day, Joy called and asked me out. We went for a drink, dinner and then she dropped me home."

Mandy smiled and I realised that was their first night together. Their first date of intimacy.

"Okay, I had never slept with anyone on my first date, but this one was different. She was irresistible. I wanted her. My body craved her touch. She embraced me and we gently kissed. I never let go again.

"Joy raised her hand and looked into my eyes; her moist soft lips were so delicate. I closed my eyes and thought it would last forever. She looked at me and understood I desired her at that moment; she walked me to my door kissing me like never before and turned the key for us to go in. I will never forget that kiss. Deep, lost in the moment, hypnotic and sensual yet tender and mesmerising. Joy had me in the moment. I have had partners before, but no one like her. She takes my breath away.

"We had spoken, flirted and gotten to know each other. When Joy started to make love to me I felt completely comfortable, relaxed. There was no awkwardness.

"We went in to my house and I poured two glasses of wine? Did you know the kitchen is one of the best places to have sex? I read it in an article in

Andrea Aviet

Cosmopolitan. And oh yes, trust me it is." She fixed me with earnest eyes.

"While I poured the red wine, Joy came up to me from behind. She had dimmed the lights and started to rub her hands on my hips. She explored my curvaceous figure, slid her hands down the side of my legs and under my skirt making her way up into my thin black stockings. She slid her hands further up into my lace underwear where she started to rub me gently, slowly. She rubbed a little more vigorously until I leaned back, resting on her. While my back rested on her chest she started to undo the buttons of my white top, one by one, exposing my white lace bra. She fondled my breast gently. It felt good. I could not move. Joy guided me round to face her and kissed me. I undid her shirt, loosened her belt and pulled down the zip on her jeans.

"Clothes were a hindrance and I could not wait to get rid of them all, just so that we could have naked flesh on flesh. I wanted to feel the warmth of her naked body under my black satin sheets. As fast as my trembling hands could, I undressed her while we kissed. We unwrapped each other, lost in the moment. Joy took the lead. She was amazing. After she had explored every inch of my body, she leaned forward to get two pillows. She slid them under my behind. She started to rub my outer labia. She moved on to my clitoris before giving me oral. We had a crazy first night, from spooning, to 69, to vibrators and gentle bondage, including whips. I cannot tell you that we did not go full on. The pleasure unbelievable; she brought on the best orgasm I have ever had and hit my G-spot."

As Mandy spoke her voice began to quiver. It was completely evident that Joy was a great partner in bed and able to perform well. In fact, the way she spoke and described Joy made me start to crave sex, although I knew nothing about lesbian sex. I had agree that it was an art which, like any other sexual encounter, needed skill and practise. After all this talk I needed an ice-cold shower to suppress my raging hormones. But instead, I asked Mandy some more questions, despite my better judgement.

Curiosity got the better of me.

"Do you use lubricants?"

Mandy told me that her sex drive, and Joy's, was that good they never needed anything besides seeing one another in a room. That was enough to spark them off.

"We are into each other, but yes, in the past sometimes we have watched good porn. However, we try not to watch a lot because it's easy to get addicted to the world of fantasy, it's like entrapment. What people fail to understand is that porn stars are professional actors playing upon your deepest and wildest fantasy. They dig deep into the subconscious parts of your darkest desires and bring them to surface, alive and in your face. The so-called love making scenes are enactment for monetary gain. They are not real."

Have you heard the groans, the moans? They're so over the top. And theire lies the problem. Many couples or partners fail to realise it's all put on to attract the average every day customers. Those who get so obsessed can get angry with their partners who don't react in the same way as the porn star did. Those who get so obsessed with roleplay that the lines between reality and fantasy get blurred and many lose themselves to the world of fantasy. Since that perfect scream, that perfect expression, just like the actor/actress is never achieved, many a relationship breaks down. Naturally when you chase after fiction and games, you stand to lose the real deal which is right in front of you. Fantasy at this point transforms into the state of desired perfectionism.

"I miss Joy, I love her. I love the way she makes me feel. I love the way she cares, the way she always reminds me about stuff and never fails to remember a special occasion. She organises surprises, kind gestures. These are the few but important things which made me fall in love with her."

For the first time in my life I actually understood that 'love is love'.

People may criticise that which does not fall into the 'normal' bracket. We might judge, we might put down or discriminate against things that we don't really understand.

Yet what was special regarding the bond between Mandy and Joy? In their own way and preference, it was a love and a relationship that they had established.

After getting to learn from Mandy about the art of love making between same sex partners I further discovered it was all about desire, satisfaction, wants and achieving that comfort zone with someone who you could call your own.

Is that not what we all look for? Love, acceptance, comfort, passion and fulfilment of our every need along with stability? The ability to rely on someone else to hold you up should you fall. Someone to comfort you in sorrow and to share your success in times of prosperity.

"Why are you so upset with Joy?"

"Well, it's our anniversary and I had planned this big event to make Joy's fantasy become a reality. But I could not take her going off with someone else."

Andrea Aviet

"Did you know, when you first got together, that Joy was bisexual?"

"Yes," she replied.

"Well did you not realise that if you gave her, her fantasy she would act upon it?"

Mandy was quiet; realistically she knew it was like dangling a bone in front of a dog. Human nature and instinct would be to grab temptation with both hands and not let go. That's exactly what Joy did. We need to accept each other for who we are, not just love the parts we want to. If your partner is telling you who they are, what they are like, accept the totality, not just a fragmented part of them and build your relationship on that part. It doesn't work like that. Mandy wanted to deny a certain part of Joy's nature; she was aware of it. She wanted to gift her her fantasy, but could not follow through because, unrealistically, she wished that Joy would just focus on her alone. I told Mandy that I thought she was being unfair to Joy.

Never try to change a person. Time after time we see so many people trying to change each other, which is when complications occur. Acceptance is the key to understanding that you can change yourself, your situation, but you are not in control of changing the lives of others.

"I ruined it, didn't I?"

Opaque Desires

My silence was an acknowledgement that she might be right.

I had to call in sick and get some sleep.

Mandy tried to lay her hand on mine; gently apologising. But all I could offer her was friendship, my time, spare bed and nothing else.

Andrea Aviet

7th August – The best sex with confidence

I climbed into bed, lay my head on my pillow and covered myself gratefully with a sheet. Bed at last. I'm sure I fell asleep as soon as my head hit the pillow. The bed just felt so comfortable.

After awhile of blissful slumber, I became aware of someone massaging my back. After such a long day, and then an equally long night, I did not question that a back massage was something I desperately needed. I just lay there, enjoying it. It was Tom, my best friend. He heard from another colleague at work that I had called in sick. He came to check up on me and Mandy had let him in.

"Are you okay?"

"Yes, just drained."

He continued to rub my back. Without opening my eyes, I asked him to stay with me. I didn't feel like being alone. Maybe that was not such a good idea, as Tom had always had a soft spot for me.

He stayed and watched over me. It was noon when I woke up to find that Tom was lying next to me in bed. He had been watching me sleep and there was

no sign of Mandy. Tom loved going to the gym and was really fit, but he was a friend. I didn't want any complications so I kept him at arm's length.

"Mandy left a while ago. She went to check up on Joy while I watched you sleep. You looked so calm and beautiful. Like an angel."

He asked how I felt and went to the kitchen to make me a drink. I wasn't ready to get out of bed; it was going to be a lazy and have a rest day. It's not often one gets to have a nice lazy day. So why not make the most of it? Hopefully there would be no more crisis calls or friends needing me to rescue them. It was time for me to catch up on my rest.

As I was imagining my lazy day, Tom returned with a tray. He took me by surprise. He had made brought me breakfast: buttered toast and salmon. There was a cup of coffee with milk and no sugar, just the way I like it. On the centre of the tray stood my little flower vase with one rose which was always kept on my kitchen counter. The presentation, though simple, looked sweet. I mentally gave him 100 points for effort.

"Come on sleeping beauty, I have brought you breakfast in bed."

I couldn't help but smile. Let me be clear: this pleased my heart, but why? Because it was not something I was accustomed to. It felt good to be treated right, the way a man is supposed to treat a woman; spoil her, show her she has value and is not just there for sex. She needs to be respected and appreciated. Breakfast never tasted this good before.

Many men forget how to treat their woman. Why is that? Why do men not go out of their way all the time to create an impression and impress? Why do we women come off as easy to get into bed?

Realising at that moment, the biggest issue is not only about female partners, but all partners irrespective of gender. There is one basic rule; you have to have confidence and self-respect. Many of us crave love. That is the reason we lose ourselves in the process. When we find that special person who gives us attention and devotes their time, we become bewitched under their influence. They shower affection upon you. We like feeling cared for; it puts us in touch with our feminine side.

On the other hand, weak knees, racing emotions and irrational decisions lead to many follies. Sometimes, you get so wrapped up in that person that you forget your own life, needs, desires. Everything starts to revolve around your other half. You find yourself changing because the other person likes you a certain way. Yet that's not you. You want to experience that continuous interest, the ongoing affection. But often, all that is new feels perfect. With time and a deeper understanding, often comes the truth of relationship and cracks can begin to show. Those cracks, previously concealed, now become more visible. First impressions always create a special, unforgettable moment in time.

Are we giving our partners the desired fuel to empower us and keep the motivation going? The key is confidence. Build on it, recognise your positives, enhance upon them and walk away. Walking away is good generally a good strategy, even if you intend to return. It helps you choose the rubbish from the good, helps you segregate the worthy from the worthless.

A confidant person will be self-reliant. Their beauty lies within their own perception of themselves. The will be content to be who they are, and appreciate their own physical, mental and emotional self. They stand on their own with pride, self-respect and cannot be influenced to change themselves, unless the desire to change stems from within. There is something very appealing about a person who can hold their own. Strength of character has a beauty, second to none. It was this quality of confidence that I had. Tom was very positive and confident. He needed a woman who would challenge him, not try to rule or control him. He needed someone who he could be himself with.

Andrea Aviet

Over breakfast, Tom said, "There is nothing worse than a negative woman who lacks confidence in herself."

I understood this completely, because when you deal with negativity, it's a continuous battle to stay on top and make it work. Not only does it drain your energy level but it creates stress between couples. Tom told me that he loved being around me because of my personality. Personally, I would concentrate on surrounding myself with positive people only.

Negativity stems mainly from fear, anxiety and a lack of self-worth. It can have a massive impact on a person's happiness, too. An unhappy mind will cause you to act and speak negatively, not only about your own life but about that of others as well. I'm a strong believer in the power of maintaining a positive mindset and focusing on speaking positive words. When you maintain a can-do attitude, every desire of your heart will be dealt with in a positive way. Having a partner who shares the same attitude and belief is a rare gem.

Tom responded to the positivity in me. He told me it was a refreshing change to find a woman who could hold her own. Now this made me smile. I was still in bed and he was *so* good looking.

Damn it, he's cute, I thought to myself. He was well-built, had an olive complexion, hazel coloured eyes, black hair and towered above me at 6' tall. I couldn't say I'd had too much to drink and use that as an excuse to make a move. But having spoken about sex so much in the recent days, my hormones were working on overdrive. Confident men don't shy away from their desires. Tom kissed me. I think he was testing the waters, and I made no gesture to stop him. He saw the green light and came back for more. Why not succumb to a steamy afternoon of sex? He was amazing. He kissed and teased, building desire; he slid his lips across my abdomen and let his wet tongue run up from navel to my breast. He tugged gently at my bedsheets and removed my satin nightgown. What lay before him was like a naked canvas for him to paint and apply his touch. He had a talent for sex, there's no denying it. He could hit the right spot deep within me, as he glided in and out slowly, progressing fast, faster and slowly teasing again. I bit lip as he reached for my hands. Once again he increased his speed as our fingers entwined.

His self-control and pacing were utter perfection. The sheets on the bed were tossed aside as desires of the flesh ruled and action justified pleasure. We tried it all. Trust me when I say I had no need to hit the gym that day. My work out was on Tom. He enjoyed me straddling and riding him. He held my breasts as I leaned forward to kiss him. He loved when I leaned backwards holding his feet for support, arching my back.

We talked, shared our desires and made our every fantasy come alive. Now that's what makes a good session of sexual fulfilment, leaving you satisfied for many days to come. No shyness, no awkwardness and no criticism. Just pure confidence in the way you look and feel. Confidence in yourself, knowing that you're good at what you do and knowing exactly what you require from your partner too. Being open and frank about your expectations helps, as partners are not mind readers. If you don't ask, then you don't get, it's as simple as that.

Tom told me that this was the best experience he had ever had. He wanted to know if this was a one off or could we have a replay.

"Well, it depends on when I start to have my sexual cravings again, it's as simple as that," I replied with a smile.

He started to laugh.

"That's what I love about you. You're not afraid to be upfront, straightforward, transparent and confident. You know exactly what you want and when. I love being with a woman who knows exactly what she wants."

Remember my advice, my friends. Whether it is a husband, wife, girlfriend, boyfriend or friend with benefits, confidence in loving yourself is the key to everything in life. You've got to love yourself first before you love anyone else. You come first. Never try to change to satisfy anyone else because when you are no longer in that relationship it will all have been for nothing. Change only if you desire to change. For yourself, alone.

Lying on my bed I felt a new level of energy. I felt refreshed, as if the tiredness had left my body. It is believed that good intercourse is the best form of exercise one can have. Well after what I just experienced, I wasn't going to argue about that.

At 5pm, I decided it was time to get out of bed and have a bath. A lovely hot, scented bubble bath with some music playing was just what I needed to make my day amazing. Getting out of bed with nothing but the black satin sheet draped around my body, I heard a knock on the door. I opened the door to find the postman standing there. He smiled, perhaps he thought he was going to get lucky?

I signed for the parcel and stood waiting for him to hand it over.

"Could I have my parcel please?"

"Oh, I'm so sorry. Yes of course. Here. You're just... so beautiful." The postman handed me my parcel.

Andrea Aviet

I blushed and whispered a thank you as I shut the door.

7th August – I love me (cont)

As I climbed into the steaming bath, I caught a glimpse of my naked self in the mirror. I told myself 'honey, you look good girl. You're just right.'

At 34, about to turn 35, I was aging well. I had a nice ass, slender but not thin, smooth skin, small but firm breasts. Then I looked at myself more closely. Was there anything I would like to change about me? Not really, there was nothing. During my younger days I wished I looked like a supermodel. As I've grown older and wiser, I do look like a supermodel when I'm wearing my make up, and so does a super model. I wished in my teenage days that I was tall with slender legs to walk the run way. Everyone used to comment that I had the face but not the height. I'd walked the run way amongst a group of tall models a few years back and I was picked out for my beautiful face. Eva Longoria is short but gorgeous and she's a model and an actress. I wished to have large breasts until I saw some of the most beautiful woman in the world were flat-chested. I saw some other people in the world without arms or legs; others had their breasts removed due to illness.

How blessed I was to have the perfect figure for me, and that's all that matters. It matters how I see myself, not the way others see me. To appreciate and love one's self is, first and foremost, most important. From self-acceptance and self-love stems self-appreciation.

Have you ever taken note of someone who does not have confidence in themself? They need approval from any and everyone for the way they look, where they go, what they eat. The indecisiveness and mental confusion they battle in themself when having to make decisions, is unimaginable.

I soaked luxiouriously in the back and a sudden memory resurfaced. I remembered going to the pub to meet some friends a few weeks back. While I waited, I noticed another young girl standing at the bar next to me. Her frame was large and she looked stunning. Another lady approached the bar. She was in a wheelchair and had no legs. Yet, what stood out about her was her confident persona; she emitted a kind of radiance. She had a magnetic personality and was soon surrounded by her friends. She seemed to be the light and focus of attention. Not as someone needing care, but as an equal part of the group. Her confidence was literally visible. She was truly beautiful. When I looked at her I saw inspiration, a person's aspirations in not limiting themselves because they have special needs, not feeling sorry for what they did not have but accepting and embracing all that they have. Her memory made me smile, I don't know who she was, but I carry her positivity with me to this day.

I decided to have an early night. It had been a very hectic phase in my life and now I just felt the need to take it easy and rest. To catch up on some much needed me time. In the world today, everything keeps happening at such a fast pace that we just don't have enough quality time to ourselves. We get caught up in daily activities, there is something always to do, always something happening. Life as we know it is a continuous circle. We are in a never-ending race to fulfil commitments on every level, be it professional or personal. But when do we fulfil our own private commitments and refuse to neglect ourselves, we reap the benefits. It's easier said than done, but simply put, we just need to stop, take a deep breath and say, "I come first; the rest will have to wait."

This step is so simple, but hard to follow. To put everything on hold until you deal with yourself first, can leave you feeling selfish. Yet if you're not going to have love for yourself who else will?

This is exactly what most of my friends lacked in their own lives. I wished for self-realisation to dawn upon them, and open up their eyes to reality.

Andrea Aviet

8th August – True love never dies.

Sunday was coming around again. I'd promised my friend that I would go with her to her church. I had been brought up to believe in God, yet church had never appealed to me. I found the services to be long, boring and definitely not interesting. Now at this late stage in my life, in the name of friendship, I agreed to attend.

I walked in trying to keep an open mind.

Did I really want to be there? Not at all. It was going to be no different from the countless other services I'd attended and hated. My mind was made up.

As we entered the church, I was very surprised to see such a small gathering. I could easily count the number of people there and noticed everyone's faces as they turned to greet us. That's when a radiant little lady came up to me, smiling.

"Hello and welcome to our church," she said.

I was taken aback by the friendliness, the likes of which I had never experienced before in any other church. Then I learnt that the lady who greeted me so warmly was none other than the pastor of that church. It was a big Methodist church.

We sang quite a few hymns, which I enjoyed. I didn't join in because I felt awkward about putting my hands up and dancing too. I know there is no shame in worshipping the loving Father above, yet when you're not brought up in a certain way, it quite difficult to get accustomed to at first.

This little lady amazed me again. She stood up and, before she ministered, welcomed each and every one individually for coming to the church and praising God. I know some congregations are too large to do that, yet a collective mention of appreciation is seldom given either.

It was lovely to see how humble, down to earth and welcoming she was to the people. Later, I discovered the most beautiful meaning behind the phrase 'true love'. Let me share with you.

Every Sunday this lady preacher would show up and smile. I watched her. Every birthday or festival a card would arrive in the post with all good wishes. I felt she had a love which was pure and hard to define, until one day I heard the heartbreaking and sensationally gripping story about true love.

One day after mass the pastor's wife had gone out for lunch with her sister-in-law and her daughter. They simply wanted to relax and have a good ladies' day out. All of a sudden, a call from her son disturbed their little gathering.

"Mum come home, Mum come home now. The police are here."

The pastor's wife's sister-in-law drove them home as quickly as she could, feeling within her heart that something had happened to her brother. She felt it. The daughter started to cry in the car.

"It can't be," said the pastor's wife. "Nothing could have gone wrong with my beloved."

When they got home, the police started to address the pastor's wife. Her husband had been involved in an accident and had died.

She was struck in utter dismay and shock; no words could be spoken, no response heard. In front of her very eyes, in just a few moments her life had turned to devastation and ruin. Just like shattered glass smashing on the floor, dropped from a great height with a shrill, shattering sound, her life exploded in tiny pieces and scattered to the four corners.

Her life had lifted her right up, blessed her with a loving man and a happy marriage. But the cruelty of fate brought her right down to her knees. Darkness, loss, tragedy had stolen from her the joy, peace and love she had felt. It had stolen her inner light. Now, all she felt was gloom and doom.

Where self-love is lost and life ceases to hold any importance, existence becomes meaningless, a habit of the living dead wherein you breathe, but long to be with your beloved. To hear his voice, to touch his hand, to share a laugh and look into his face. What would she give to speak the words "I love you from within the depths of my soul, good bye my love safe journey to the other side. I will miss you and forever I carry you wherever I go, within my heart for as long as I live till the day we are together gain."

In the weeks and months to follow, she had many a silent conversation with her husband from a very broken heart to his peaceful spirit. "Why my love? Why dear lord? How will I cope? My world is lost; I am drowning and want to be left alone in the darkness for the rest of time."

Yet God had plans. We cannot know His plans happen. Nor does man know the reasons behind mysterious circumstances and the outcome they lead us to.

But out of the darkness came strength. Out of the loss came unity and leadership in the name of true love. An anointment of a new leadership, so that lost souls would not stray, but so that generations to come would be saved and the souls of many comforted in times of trial and tribulation. Out of sorrow came new birth. The pastor made the transition from the stage of losing one's self, to the grief carried by a wife, to rebuilding one's self with the prayers of the faithful few. Family and friends stood by her side and helped with the children. Out of these trials and tribulations emerged a strong, beautiful, powerful servant of God to lead people, but for the sake of true love. Her lover, her partner, her husband, her everything had put his heart and mind into running the church.

We talk of love, we speak our mind out aloud that we crave that one perfect love affair and if we had it we would never let it go. Well what about when you find it but it's snatched away from you? Does the love still go on? Do you carry it with you or do you move on? These are the various thoughts which came to my mind?

In my quest for the various aspects of love, sex, relationships and insight?

Learning from the pastor's wife, who soon took on the role of being a pastor to carry on the legacy of her husband, I viewed her story as love being carried on and never dying. She keeps alive the memory and the love she carries inside by still walking by his side in the spirit. She goes against her very own desire to give up all, but sacrifices for him and takes on what he would have done. In the flesh, if he were present. He, in return, looks down from above and says, "Do not cry my beloved. Long have we been together and soon shall we be again. Your journey has not ended and you are still needed by our people, by our children and by our grandchildren. Do not cry for me, for I am with the Father. One day my love together we will all be, at the end in paradise where love never dies but lives forever. Until then my love, remember me. Until then, I see you and love you all. The love never dies, the void never replaced or filled, I carry you up above like you carry me from down below. I hear your heart, Jesus answers your prayers, I feel your love in the good you do for my people. Soon we will be together again. Soon, my love. Until then, hold on, you're doing great. With all my love your husband, friend and lover."

True love never dies; the memory lives on within you.

This is the story of the greatest love affair I have ever witnessed across the natural earthly plane and the supernatural, heavenly paradise. From up above to down below, the bond of love flows eternally.

I found myself asking, once again, "What about the physical love? The need for physical affection between couples? At the end, what matters?"

When old age strikes your body, parts of it don't function that well, even though desire may still prevail. In your youthful days you may have been a stallion. Yet in years to come your vigour fizzles out.

Andrea Aviet

What is it that keeps the relationship going?

Companionship, mutual understanding, respect, true love where beauty never dies and wrinkles show the longevity of time well spent together. Who can say that true love does not exist? Have you ever found it? I have not but I have seen it among a special few who have. It does not differentiate between colour, race, physique, language, culture, ethnicity, geographical barriers or gender. Rather it breaks all boundaries. Love builds, it does not destroy. Love creates and uplifts, it elevates you to new heights and makes a beautiful bond between two souls.

How blessed are those to find this precious gift of love? For what is life without love?

I have sometimes seen, while walking about, a couple who in my wildest of dreams I would not have ever imagined to be together. Yet taking a closer look at them, I see that they have withstood the test of time. Their eyes still twinkle with delight when they are in each other's company. Facial expressions speak more than words. Even in the silence of their own company there is still music, even without words spoken their heartbeats speak to each other. Love does not need words. Love is care, love is companionship and love is mutual respect and unity.

I have noticed that in their every action, their gentle touch and reaction there is a unique delicacy. So amazing is the bond of heartfelt emotion, so elevating. Life as we know it was not meant to be lived alone, but shared. Either with someone who is truly special or someone who is your true soulmate. A love so unique which does not look at size, colour and wealth. The transitional stages of attraction, desire, lust, passion, pleasure and sexual hunger are what we all go through to find the 'one'. Your other half who will excite you, be by your side, make love to you by night and stand by your side by day.

Spending time together helps you understand the unspoken words of love. With the passing of the years, your once robust hands change to feeble, lined, wrinkled hands. But still you hold each other closer than ever before and utter the words 'I love you'. Standing in front of the mirror you see the older you, but the love inside has withstood the test of time. When you glance in the mirror memories come rushing back of youthful mischief and resounding laughter.

As you turn to look at your lover through the wrinkles, you can see the sparkle in his eyes which never fades. The exterior has withered, while the interior is still intact. The heart still beats and the love still grows for you. Time has strengthened your love.

Andrea Aviet

That's the love my heart desires. A lover who will hold me close, now and forever, as we journey through the abyss of time, making our own history together.

While I myself was in no hurry to rush into a relationship for the wrong reasons, I am still human and crave pleasures of the flesh that intrigue me from time to time. It is human nature that desire rules. Emotions and lack of satisfaction leads to cravings. Being starved of sexual desires can sometimes lead to many a folly. Time reveals and brings forth all good, it even allows mistakes and then has a way of letting things rectify themselves in due course.

16th August – The financial killer

Yet, I see some friends who start a love affair and, in time, resign themselves to settling down together because of convenience. When the newness of the love has worn off, the excitement has ceased, and being a part of each other is neither celebrated nor is the passion kept alive. Many a relationship runs into common, mundane problems. Like having lack of money, leading to restrictions on leading the lives we want. Sadly, instead of working together to support and build upon changing needs, couples can turn on each other under pressure and cracks start to appear in their relationship.

Ted and Mai were a fantastic couple. Both came to London in their early teens and decided to go into the hospitality business. Both were excellent at what they did and truly gifted professionals in their respective fields. After a while they decided to live together. They had developed a mutual attraction and bond of love. The love lasted and it was good; they were good together. They worked together to build their dreams, bolster their ambitions and work on their careers. But as their little family unit started to grow, things began to change. When it was just them as a couple it was fine. The commitment was there but the life was not so filled with responsibility and the pressure was manageable. However, like many other couples they decided to embark upon a new journey – family life. Plans were being made and, knowing they had the financial stability to back them up, they ploughed ahead with their plans. They had the security of having their own home, they were paying for a mortgage.

I find it advisable, at this stage of life, to have a mutual check list drawn up, with agreements and disagreements, outlining what each one is ready to do in the partnership, to prevent complications further down the line. This can help both partners understand what they can and can't commit to doing.

Every couple takes it as the next step in their relationship to have a child but we should think seriously about it. It is the nature of every traditional society to expect partners to enter at some point into a progressive state of becoming a parent. Parenthood is seen as climbing up the staircase of society, forming a family hierarchy. But are you yourself ready to be a parent? Is your partner ready to be a parent? Or are you just doing it because it's what society expects from couples? Do you have time for all the family commitments, late nights, untidy houses, crying, chasing after the children, sleepless nights? It involves after the kids, staying up when they cannot sleep, staying up when they are ill, and running to school, changing your timings to suit theirs, being available during school holidays. Providing not only a roof over their head, but quality time to spend with them.

Are you ready for the entire package? The psychological, emotional, mental demands? And providing a happy, safe, joyful family atmosphere for all within the household?

Let me tell you, Ted and Mai thought they were ready too.

Their intensions were noble yet they lacked precise understanding. Deciding to bring a life into the world, to join the family together and become parents is very precious. However, when you lack insight it can be the hardest of things to follow up on. And then life starts to become a struggle, not because you cannot manage, but simply because you lack the 'know how.' Sadly, before they had the kids, the house was clean and neat, before the kids they worked hard and partied harder during the weekend. If they wanted to travel they would save up and just fly off somewhere romantic, somewhere interesting. They never gave much thought to their plans. But now life had changed drastically. They no longer had the lives of a single couple. They were now mummy and daddy.

Employees and parents. When work ended the second job took over as soon as they stepped through the front door. They lacked rest, 'me time, 'us time'. The lack of any time at all started to take its toll on the two, and their love was put to the test. Ted and Mai's relationship stood the test of time in one way. They are still together in name alone. They are held together by the bond of materialistic valuables and show for society. I see Mai working hard professionally, but when she returns home, she is tired. She still has to work hard in the house, look after the kids and do everything else. Whereas Ted is most relaxed. He pressurises Mai to take on all the responsibility. I would not do that because it would mean being silent just to keep the peace behind closed doors. I would like my partner, husband and father of my children to help actively and take an equal part in everything we do as a couple, from the start to the very end.

Watching them both closely shocked me one day. How did they turn so awful together? Most couples lose themselves under stress, pressure at work and take it out on each other at home. Most start to bicker and argue with each other instead of taking their frustrations out on their superiors or colleagues. Stress is turned upon family members, which is both neither ethical nor morally right.

When children act out of character, it's mostly because they are being influenced negatively, somewhere by someone. They are very intelligent and watch everything, hear every conversation spoken, process and in act out what they see. I could see that their perfect family unit had fine flaws and cracks. But it is not for outsiders to point out the mistakes you make. It is for you yourself to recognise and rebuild. Work on your relationship for the good of the entire family unit. I recognised certain behaviour which I did not like. Ted was being inconsiderate and every time he got upset, Mai would get the brunt of it.

But why? She too had her stress, so I concluded that he took the easy way out.

If I was Mai I would simply give Ted an ultimatum or walk away and start afresh. The questions of realisation once again needed to be asked. Do I want the house and car or do I want a happy peaceful home? Do I want an abundance of money with all the stress and anxiety it carries, or do I want less money, fewer worries but a happy home?

A home where love, laughter and happy memories prevail. A home where stability and peace are present.

It was their decision to make. Whether to continue or to go their separate ways. To change for the better or end their relationship. Many couples don't understand that the love inside does not die, but changes. We grow together yet we must not let domination take over our senses.

The relationship needs to be worked on, because, when children come on to the scene it does not mean you don't enjoy your time together. Arranging for a babysitter or a romantic getaway dinner is a must. You simply cannot put your relationship on the line, you cannot let the love fizzle out and die.

Sex needs to continue. It needs to be spiced up. Dress up as a bar maid, dive into your sexual fantasies and bring them back up to the surface. Fun helps to excite life and fuel romance. Will a partner want to return to misery or will a partner want to return to a hot, steamy, sexy other half, fulfilling their every fantasy?

I asked Mai one day, after I saw the children shouting at each other, what was the cause of such behaviour? Where do they pick this type of behaviour up from?

"I don't like it, but they pick it up at home."

"When was the last time you and Ted had any adult alone time?"

They had not had any time alone together in a very long time, so what do you expect? Sex is a natural stress buster. As well as making you feel good, it energises a relationship and invites excitement back into a bond. It's not difficult; all that matters is how much you desire something to work out, without compromising your own life's needs.

Mai needed to sort them out. If Ted was not stepping up to the mark, she needed to for the sake of the innocent pairs of eyes who watched the examples set by their parents. What would they learn about love, parenting, adulthood? It all stems from home. The grounding you install in your little ones will be deep rooted in them as individuals when they lead their own lives.

Why do some individuals not respect their partners and treat them as trash? Look deeper. Dive into their upbringing, location and character of the surrounding society in that geographical area. Look at the values, ethnicity and religion. There is a much greater influence than people realise and understand. They play an active part in shaping and formulating the family structure.

Mai and Ted had money, the big car, the big house, so financial stability existed and persisted. However, they managed to maintain a family unit that lacked unity.

Unfortunately, being caught up in the show of perfectionism and the show of maintaining what they had, they started to part ways. Leading Mai to take on more than she could handle to keep the peace. But all she wanted to do was get up and leave. Yet pride would not let her walk away. Love for a proper and happy family life led her to continue, lost. The only way she felt she could continue was by becoming subdued, listening to him continuously. However, I feel it would have been better, for the sake of the children, if they could not resolve the issues between them, to just walk away.

How badly do you want to pursue happiness? How hard are you willing to try to make your relationship work? Beware: it takes two to tango; you can't do it on your own.

Many of us go wrong when we start to become that desperate to make something work that it turns into a dependency. A need to stay with the other person because you just get so used to having that person around, you feel you cannot cope without them. It's silly really, because it's all in your mind. The fear of loneliness, the fear of not being able to cope or manage, the anxiety. It's all a part of your imagination. But you need to focus, be brave, have self-belief and realisation about what you can do. You'er stronger than you realise, even if your back's up against the wall.

You're stronger, if you only believe in yourself. I am a strong believer in mind over matter and removing the negative influences which weigh you down. Negativity is simply not worth it, and life is too precious. Have you ever noticed people, when they get so caught up in the show of everything, that they themselves become actors? All their reactions are a pretext based upon what others expect of them. The fake fabrications and portrayal of a perfect, happy, family life, which is put on to show the world. Who are they trying to fool? Is it the friends who have witnessed the chaos? Strangers? Or is it just from themselves they hide? Are they just trying to persuade their own conscience that life is perfect, because we live together under one roof?

Yet Mai must find her own way. Until she's ready, no amount of good advice will be considered. Sometimes you need to sit back and wait. When it's time to help and the situation arises, then you can offer help. Until then, from a back seat in the distance, love and support can be offered whenever needed.

Andrea Aviet

19th August – Sex addiction

Those are the tough facts of life.

And now it was time for me to head back into work. After all, one has to work to pay the bills and live a somewhat decent life. Work was always a pleasure for me. The mixture of workmates I had was diverse and fascinating. It was not only a place of work, but a place of stimulation. Some of the stories I would hear after the weekend were not only funny but intriguing. The sex a couple had, was it good? The group sex, when someone could not get it up and had left the lady wanting , unsatisfied. So, meeting up with my younger colleagues after the weekend was something I often looked forward to.

Ramsey was the first of my colleagues I spoke to. Maybe I should call him a playmate! He was so addicted to pornography that we joked that he would always have to play with himself, since no woman could ever live up to his fantasies. Or if he found one, she would have to be a blow-up doll. Ramsey's doll was called Jess. He loved it, especially since it was a present for his 40th birthday. He also had another hidden addiction: he loved to call sex chat lines. It got so intense that he would spend all his money on phone sex. Eventually, what started as an innocent curiosity had turned into a compelling addiction which caused him not only to fall into debt, but to owe money to any and everybody. He had arrears on his mortgage and, eventually, his house was repossessed.

What makes an intelligent man, in a well-paid job, holding down a high position, want to give up all? It hardly seems practical, nor does it seem logically possible. Yet in my life I have discovered that looks are deceptive. One should never judge another based on the norms expected by society, nor on the basis of 'normal' behaviour. As I have seen lately, what one categorises as 'normal' behaviour is often not necessarily considered normal to someone else.

Ramsey had looked rough for a few weeks. I didn't understand the extent to which he had screwed up his life. He had seemed so happy before. How could he now have such a weight on his shoulders?

He decided to confide in me. He was looking for a place to stay and, since I had plenty of friends, he asked me to point him in the right direction. First, I wanted to know everything. This is what I gathered from our brief start up conversation.

He made a call to a chat line, the number for which he'd found online. This line offered talks starting from 50p per minute. The girl of your choice would talk with you in whichever area of sex your interest lay. Ramsey's field of interest was women, so pretty much any conversation would do, as long as it was

Andrea Aviet

held with a woman. Now these lines are a trap. That evening he decided to meet me out side of work. Although I had a spare room, I made it clear he could not stay with me as it would be a temptation. his presence would be too close for my comfort.

We arranged to meet at 8pm to go out for dinner. We met at a Mexican pub just round the corner from my house. He found it difficult to open up to me. He could not relax at first and reminded me of someone who had just signed his life away. We ordered dinner and a drink to help him relax. After that he opened up a bit.

"I was lonely. There was no one there for me. I was under pressure at work and I had no time to have a social life or make plans. How pathetic, don't you think?"

"Not really," I replied. "We are professionals. All our lives are like this: fast paced, hectic. We have no time for play, just work and to make something of ourselves, that's it."

He paused and was silent. I knew Ramsey would not crack easily. Most men don't. You have to give them their time and space. When they are ready to open up they will. Until then I just had to wait. But I knew that it would be worth the wait, once he chose to open up. Patience is a virtue. Rumours in the work place had given me an insight into his lifestyle, yet I was not ready to believe hearsay. I wanted to know what he had to say for himself.

"I need help. I really can't believe how I got into all this."

Looking at him, I saw confusion, disbelief in his eyes. He was a man who had lost his vision in life. A man who needed help to find his way back.

"When you are lost, don't try to stand on your own, there is no stigma in asking good, reliable friends for support or advice. If you feel comfortable you can open up to me and I'll try my best to help you the best I can." We finished dinner and we parted ways.

A few weeks later, he failed to turn up for work. Despite my best efforts to contact him, we couldn't find him. I was worried. At any given time anyone of us can slip into a dark place where it seems impossible for even a ray of light to seep through. I prayed for him to return. Life went on and I trusted in the Father above to keep him safe, guide him in his hour of need and send comfort to his upset spirit, wherever he was.

In the meantime, I decided to sign up to work on a chat line and see what it was like. The criteria were, I had to have a good attitude, excellent communication skills and an open mind. The cost of calls varied in accordance with the times the calls were taken, and they ranged from 50p per minute, up to 60p per minute. Weekdays and weekends differed in cost, a landline was required. What attracted me were the words 'flexible working hours'. But it was no work, no pay. You had to earn a minimum of £5 per week to get paid. Of course, once you developed a 'fan base', your earnings could increase significantly. This was one place, however, that different chat lines have different rules. You had to rate the caller's desires to give you a better understanding of whether the caller just wanted a friendly conversation or was more into hard core sex. Numbers were pressed on a basis of 1 to 5 to give an indication. A unique identification number was given to each employee, by which you were known. And of course the operator made up the character they wanted to be.

I was happy that measures were taken to protect the identity on both sides, to ensure the safety of both. On the most part, the women who worked on these lines put the job down as experience in the pursuit of an acting career. It involved superficial bonding for the fulfilment of the needs of the hour. The aim was to keep them on the call for as long as possible or you risked not getting paid. You had to re-invent yourself. I got the form and filled it in, but I just couldn't bring myself to send the completed forms off. I thought about it. I went through a debate with myself, but it was not for me. Although it was the only way I could think of to help Ramsey, being honest to myself was my utmost priority.

I was upset that I couldn't go through with it. I could feel that Ramsey needed a friend to understand him, to go the extra mile for his wellbeing. In order to know someone, grasp and understand what they are going through, you have to learn from them. Walk in their shoes to get a greater insight. From a distance someone's life looks so exquisitely picture perfect. But that's exactly what it is, a picture representation. It's merely a likeness that they have painted for others to identify them by. If you come too close you might just see the uneven brush strokes and smudge marks which, from afar, look beautiful and smooth. I was devastated that I couldn't help Ramsey any further. I bumped into Zara at that point. She could tell I was upset and asked me why. I opened up to her about my failings.

Andrea Aviet

24th August – Phone sex

Zara listened carefully to every word I uttered.

"What exactly do you want to know about phone sex?"

"Everything really. It's new to me and I need to learn as much as possible about the industry to help a friend who has fallen into a vicious cycle. He can't get out of it and I don't have a clue how to help him get back on his feet".

"Why does it have to be you that helps him?"

"Because, I care."

Zara smiled. We had been friends for a long time. We were best friends, yet I discovered in the moments to follow you never actually know someone until they themselves open up to you.

"A few years ago, do you remember the banking crisis? The banks were laying staff off left, right and centre."

"Yes, I do"

"Well, during those years I was the only one working. Mack had been laid off. The redundancy money lasted only two months. Our family faced a horrific family crisis, the bills mounted, I used every

222

credit card we had and exhausted every overdraft. Finally, the house was going to be repossessed. Desperation hit so hard and we almost reached starvation point. I had to save the house. We couldn't live without a house, I had to look after the kids. I walked down some pretty dark roads. Do you have time to talk?"

In her eyes I saw a huge burden which she longed to let go of. It was weighing her down... I had to go to a meeting on behalf of my boss, but I knew it could be rescheduled. I made the call and then returned to Zara.

"Is everything alright?" she asked me, smiling.

"It is now. I've just rescheduled a meeting."

Zara thanked me; I needed to be there.

"I had reached rock bottom. We had nothing left to sell, there were bills coming in with red headlines, bailiffs knocking at our door, we'd been threatened with having our house repossessed. And my loving husband was at breaking point mentally and emotionally. I think he felt that, as the head of the family, he had let his children and wife down. It was awful, it's unbelievably cruel." Tears rolled down her face as she spoke. The pain, the sadness she felt, I felt.

Zara recalled the times when she borrowed money from everyone. There was gossip going around work that Mack was gambling and she was trying to rescue him.

"I am your best friend why did you not tell me?" I asked.

"I didn't know how to. I felt as if the walls were closing on me from all sides and I didn't know how to cope, what to do and where to turn. Please don't judge me."

"I am not," I replied. "I love you."

"Don't judge me," Zara said again, frantically. She seemed scared and alone. "I am one of them, I am an adult sex chat worker, I am also a stripper. Don't judge me, please."

Oh! Now I understood why Zara had repeated herself. It was fear of the revelation which she wanted to let out from within herself. As she said those words, she sobbed.

"I had to do it."

I cried too, as I held her and repeated my words

"I love you nonetheless. No matter what professions you chose, you did so in the name of love. You are a survivor; you are a loving mother, a dedicated wife and a home maker. You are the strength that lifts your family up from ruin, the symbol of true love and sacrifice. There is no greater love than the love of self-sacrifice in order to care for loved ones. You lost your dignity to preserve theirs. You lost your pride, to mention theirs. Who can fault you for the greatest sacrifice, which you have made in the name of family?"

Zara hugged me and would not let go.

"I love you my friend, thank you for not judging, thank you." After a while she said, "Ask me what you would like to know, I will try to help you as much as I can."

How beautiful is the human spirit? Such was Zara's nature that, in the face of hardship, diversity and darkness, she was still willing to reveal the ways of a trade she was embarrassed about, for no other reason than she may be able to help a stranger.

The love, the purity of heart and her nature was so marvellous and unique. We had to spend some more time together and so we made plans to keep meeting up for as long as it took. I set out to learn about adult chat lines. Little did I know I was also going to learn about another trade.

We met again, a few days later, and started talking. Zara is one of the most insightful people I have ever come across. We started first with the chat lines.

Andrea Aviet

"At first it was really hard. I could not get my head around it. I did not want to answer any call, yet I was reminded that I had to do this, I had to overcome my hesitation. It was a do or die situation, literally. So, it had to be mind over matter. From the beginning, I had to learn to master the trade and fast. It was all done behind closed doors and, as such, there was a strange comfort there.

"No one knew who I was. The callers could not see me, nor could I see them. It was just an act, I told myself. I was part of a play and the characters kept changing. The first call I took, the caller said I was a waste of time and money. He hung up almost instantly after I said hello.

"It wasn't easy. It was hard work. Feeling disappointed, I went onto YouTube to teach myself how to talk sexy on the phone; something I was not used to at all. In time, after each call I took, I realised it never mattered who I spoke to or what I said. As long as I kept them entertained and feeling happy that was all that mattered. To help me feel sexy, I decided to go buy some cheap, sexy underwear. That really helped me get into character.

"When I got my first pay cheque it was not a great amount, but it was a starting point to supplement the income I already had. That motivated me to

lead a more dedicated life of drama and try to earn as much as I could. So, there you have it. I played any and every part that I needed to. As long as the men stayed on the phone and I was getting paid, that was all that mattered.

"Sometimes they longed for someone to be a special character who they fancied having intercourse with. So, you have to be prepared mentally at all times. The hard facts are, you're getting paid, to stimulate someone's imagination. If the man comes off the call feeling good but bankrupt, who cares? No one forced him to keep calling. That's the attitude which persists among the people in the trade."

I thanked Zara for her time, but she stopped me.

"There's more. I reinvent my character all the time. The scariest part was, sometimes I didn't realise I was still in character and talked differently... sometimes even with my husband. I'd talk to him as one of my characters and he'd remind me 'come back to me my love...' He was always understanding, patient and caring. He knew what I was doing and why I was having to do it. He was confident in the love we share, he knew it would be tested but would never break. We had shared too much between us to let anyone or anything come between us."

Andrea Aviet

Oh, I thought, how beautiful is their love?

"Yet, because of our financial crisis I had to step up my game. It was like a vicious circle. Once you fall into debt, worry keeps bothering you continuously. That worry creeps upon you at night like a silent, persistent thief, come to steal your peace; the combination of sleepless nights and looking at the zero negative balances is too frightening.

"Late that night I told Mack, 'I love you with all my heart, but we need more money...' I found it difficult to tell Mack about my new idea. It was something I had come across in the papers. It was a strip joint opening up in our town. They were advertising for strippers and the pay was exceptionally good. The advert said to call to get more information and book an interview. I was afraid. So afraid. I had often danced in the bedroom to entertain Mack. But that was easy. He was my husband. The comfort I felt with him was at a different level; I could move and be erotic to spice up our sex life. When I told him, he was shocked, angry and stormed out without saying a word. This was the first incident in ten years where I had seen him like that.

"Hours passed and there was no sign of Mack. Worry crippled my soul. He would not take my calls. Panic gripped me, was he alright? Had he got into a fight somewhere because of me? Was my love ok?

Nearing midnight, I heard someone at the door. Mack entered and I ran to hug him.

"But he didn't hug me back. His hands stayed at his side. I knew, I just knew, I had hurt him badly. He had never needed any prompting to put his arms around my waist and hold me before. I looked him straight in the eyes, took his hand and placed it on my heart.

"'I love you with all my heart; you were there for us all, now it's my turn,' I told him. He sat down and pulled me onto his lap. He rested his head on my chest, buried between my breasts and held me. We hugged as if it was the first time we had held each other; it was so spectacular in the moment.

"'You belong to me and I belong to you,' he replied. 'The day I said 'I do, till death do us part, for better or for worse' I meant it. Each and every word of it, my wife". Tears of love rolled down my cheeks and he carried me off to bed. Slowly, passionately he kissed me. He undid my sash to the night gown and slowly made passionate love to me. It was different, so different this time. He moved within me like never before. It was special. The way he touched me, so gently, as his hand glided all over my body. It felt as if we were bonding, spiritually, in a way we had never before. Our souls were bonding together. In all the years we'd been together, that was our best ever.

Andrea Aviet

"My legs wrapped around his waist as he lifted me up and positioned himself again, penetrating gently. I was in ecstacy. Mack smiled as he put his fingers through mine 'Until the end of time, we will always stand together.'"

25th August – Strip joint

"That night was special. It gave me the strength to do what I needed to the next day. During the audition I was nervous but I remembered what my beloved said: 'Think about dancing for me. I may not be sitting in the room but remember, I sit within your heart. You're going to be fine.'

"I danced as if I danced for him, around the pole. They had auditioned and refused many women before me. But I was a yes; they asked if I had ever been a professional dancer. 'No, I have never been into the profession,' I replied. They took me on and said I had potential. They would train me to dance and strip.

"Later, they told me that my look was unique. It was not slutty, but one which was of 'innocence lost'. I was good girl turned bad. They told me I would be good for business. I had to take all my clothes off to show them I had a perfect body. One which was in good shape, fit and would draw crowds in.

"That was the hardest part. For me to go topless in front of a room of strangers while they looked at me. I thought of Mack, I thought of the kids and then I stripped off completely. all I heard was 'perfect, next please'. I ran off with clothes in my hand. As I went out I ran into Mack. It was a shock to see him there.

"'Are you okay, my love?' he asked. I clung to him, 'hold me please,' I replied.

"I felt violated but I would never share that with Mack, for he would never let me back in there. He loved me too much and I loved him. We were soul mates.

"As the days went by it got easier. The chat lines were alright in the sense that there was no physical contact with anyone. I did not see even co-workers. It was all anonymous. The strip club was completely different; there were quite a few co-workers/strippers who I made friends with. It's an entirely different environment and atmosphere. Different lives, different desires and needs.

"There was a lot more physical contact. I needed to do both jobs to recover from the financial crisis we had fallen into as a family. The system had failed us. The different paths I found on my journey for survival were nothing short of amazing. Truly eye opening. I noticed that women joined the profession for many different reasons, although it all came down to monetary gain. Bills, crises, family trouble, desperation. It is said that every coin has two sides. Likewise, the divide was between the haves and have nots. The others did not need the job as desperately as I did. But the only reason for wanting to be in the profession was to earn money quickly, effortlessly and get rich fast.

"So, it was viewed by them as an easy way out. Many of us want a quick entry into the high life style but few are willing to work for their heart's desire, the true old-fashioned way.

"All the women were highly skilled. I was a newbie, but since I had a good slender, toned, tanned and sexy physique, I fit right in. Heather was a young university student and really wanted to just rush the process of reaching the top. She was trying to save up for a house and get a deposit together. So, although we had a no hands policy, she would often try to entice them to touch her. The excitement that the possibility existed was enough to arouse every desire in them.

"That excitement led the men to stuff notes into her underwear. She often got phone numbers but never rang them. It was like playing a game to excite them, tease them and leave them wanting, craving more. She ate healthy food, looked after herself and went regularly to the gym to keep fit. After all, beauty comes at a price, and helps raise the price too."

Zara excited and aroused my interest; she agreed to introduce me to her workmates. That sounded fantastic to me. It made room for an opportunity, one within which I could feed off the knowledge of those who I desired to learn from.

The first lady I met was Heather; she was gorgeous. In a million years I would never have imagined that she was a stripper. She was tall, blonde, very fit, big busted and had a beautiful big ass. She was every man's fantasy. She represented a dream woman, her beauty surpassed all. On our first meeting she wore a pair of black leggings and a white T-shirt. Every curve in her curvaceous body was noticeable, yet she looked like a mix between a university student and a professional. She spoke with elegance and poise. I learned, after holding a conversation with her, that she supported various charities and helped many an orphanage.

Why is it then that she chose this profession? Her reasoning was that she had studied a lot and, judging from the examples set by her family members, she was not like them. Working 9 to 5 and just about making ends meet was not what she desired. Instead she wanted to capitalise on her good looks while she was young and make the very best use. She also planned to buy a house and pave the way for an early retirement. She respected the job as a professional working career, which would help her on her way to achieving her dreams. Her efforts would be well-directed, instead of being wasted fruitlessly.

She obviously spent a lot of time and money on grooming herself. When she walked into a room her beauty commanded all attention. A stress-free life helped her look more youthful. There was never any financial shortage and she had the freedom to do as she pleased, when she pleased. Heather made it a point to tell me that 'sex sells' and that I should come spend an entire day with her. I agree. Sex does sell and that was one of the reasons she did exceptionally well. She had the entire package. I just couldn't fault her. She was showing self-discipline, dedication, commitment and self-love by respecting herself on several levels. Heather told me she lives by one rule: "dream only to achieve and make your own dream a reality."

Andrea Aviet

28ᵗʰ August – Sex industry

The sex industry is based upon physical appearances: the looks, the moves and the fantasy, dramatising and capitalising on secretive, inner, passionate cravings. Exploitation of the weakness of one is someone else's strength. The strong can have power over the weak. The industry breaks through psychological perceptions to take control by arousing sexual desire. These desires act as a trigger, whereby the 'want' has to be fulfilled one way or another.

How far will you go to get what you want? Will you be able to maintain a balance between reality and fantasy? That's the trap. Most of us don't get our desires or needs met. Either our partners are not up to the mark or we are just not satisfied. It's easier, in many ways, to pay and just get what you want, when we want. But it comes at a price and nothing is free in life. Nor does it last. It is very temporary.

The next question how much? How much are you willing to pay and how far you will go? The addiction can be dangerous. The more you get, the more you want. It's never enough. Why? Because it is not free, spontaneous will, it's a dictatorship. You get exactly what you ask for; if the demands are greater the price is greater. It is only fair.

Ask yourself. Have you ever wanted your partner to do a sexy dance for you and strip? Have they done if for you? Or did they feel a certain level of discomfort? So you tell them "it's okay, never mind". But that's actually what you would have liked right?

Zara and Heather invited me to see a session of theirs; I had never been into a strip joint before. The girls were fantastic. I sat in awe as I heard the music play, the lights dimmed and Zara appeared centre stage; she was wrapped gracefully in black fur and wore black heeled shoes. Her makeup was flawless. She looked stunning. As she came on the crowds cheered. I was fascinated to see how well received she was and later, as she danced around the pole, it was like she made love to it. I loved the intriguing way and artful skill with which she slowly, seductively rubbed herself around the pole and let go of the fur, revealing her nude legs and black underwear. Her style of performance captivated the audience and it almost looked to me as if she was dancing around Mack, her husband. Zara changed my opinion about stripping. Previously, I had thought that as long as a woman danced to the music and took her clothes off, she was a stripper. Yet Zara redefined the meaning of stripping in my mind. I understood now, why men and women both came to see Zara perform. She was simply one of a kind.

As she finished, the crowd cheered and threw roses onto the stage. I smiled. She did not come off as vulgar, but artful. I would not mind dancing, just like Zara, to please my true lover, when I find him.

Next up was Heather; the blonde beauty looked every bit like Pamela Anderson. The resemblance was strikingly shocking. She was completely different, and although she was just as seductive as Zara, the style of stripping was different.

She dressed as a business lady and then stripped of. Her strong, athletic frame was very well received by the crowd. The performance had cat calls, whistles, cheers; it was completely different from Zara's. The high level of energy and enthusiasm was admirable. She was fit and her strength spoke volumes about the care she took. Heather managed to rouse the calmest of crowds; whip them up into a frenzy. She was an instigator and urged people to show their feelings.

I needed to ask them both whether they ever developed feelings for the people they saw on a regular basis. Both women agreed that you develop familiarity but have to always keep in mind that this is nothing more than a profession. As such, you should separate the two. Keep the professional performance away from the personal aspect. The combination of the two can only lead to ruin of one's own career.

Both woman were in the same profession, yet they so different in every way. It just goes to show you nothing is the same, everyone has their own style and is uniquely different. I thanked both ladies kindly for letting me into their world and showing me a day in the life of a stripper, and sharing with me the other activities they were involved with.

The demand for the sex industry in every capacity runs into the millions. I had gained a much-needed personal experience with the ladies but now it was time to return home. We had enjoyed our new bond of friendship and soon I would visit the strip joint for no other reason than to visit my friends.

Andrea Aviet

1st September – Rescue me

I was happy that day. I was walking back home from work, when I noticed a man sitting on the pavement, under a tree. He wore nice shoes, but was draped in a sheet and he sat with his head in his hands. It started to rain, a heavy downpour, so I ran into a nearby coffee shop to take shelter. I looked back at the man, wondering what his story was. I ordered myself a coffee and sat at the table near the window, where I had a good view of the entire street. The rain fell and, as the cars passed, they splashed through the water which was quickly filling up the sides of the road. My attention returned to the man with the nice shoes. Was he a beggar? Was he still alive? The rain poured down. I decided not to move. I was only wearing heels and a thin strappy white dress. I'd left my umbrella at home, not expecting rain today. There was no way I was going to venture out until the rain stopped. Coffee was my companion and the little shop was crowed because everyone wanted shelter from the downpour.

Around 10 minutes later, I looked up when I heard a loud noise. A lady shouted "look out!" from behind me. The people in the shop had all stopped their conversation and were staring, terrified, at a group of boys with bats in their hands. They appeared to be a group of young college boys and a little drunk.

They were standing over the man with the shoes. It seemed that they wanted to have a little fun. One of them hit the bin to make the man, sat next to it, jump. He did not budge. The others stood around watching, laughing, cheering him on. The boy wanted a reaction but there was none. He decided to go one step further.

The boy lifted his bat and struck the man across his back. This made the soaked sheet fly off. Oh, my heart was in my mouth. The other boys stood to one side and cheered him on. The lady from the coffee shop ran to the door and shouted across to leave the man alone. With the door open, none of us could hear each other. The rain and the thunder were too loud. As the beggar got up, I saw his face briefly. My God, it was Ramsey.

"Oh no!" I shouted in the shop. "Help me! That's my missing friend."

Either it was extreme foolishness or courage, I don't know under which, but I ran as fast as I could, towards Ramsey. I dodged in between traffic, through the rain and thunder.

"Stop!" I shouted, running in front of the boys and in front of Ramsey. The boy looked at me and shouted at me to leave. Before I knew it, others from the coffee shop had gathered behind the boy and were telling him that he was the one who should leave. Faced with a crowd, the boys ran back to their car and drove off quickly; I thanked all who stood by my side. This was greatest act of love and humanity. Bonding to save someone helpless. The gathered crowd soon dispersed in the pouring rain, but I was grateful to them all.

Turning to Ramsey, I hugged him. He did not look like himself. He looked rough. He said thank you and tried to walk away.

"Just stop," I called after him. "I have searched for you and worried for weeks. You're coming with me." We walked together in the thunder, in the rain, we were both drenched. My thin, summer clothes clung to my body and nothing was left to imagination. I did not care. There was a certain level of peace I had found in finding Ramsey and I was not going to let him out of my sight. He just kept glancing at me silently; I cannot even pretend to know what he thought or what he was going through at that moment in time. A few minutes down the street and we were at my home. I told him to come up; he looked at me silently and then asked if I was sure.

"Come up, I insist."

We walked up the stairs. When I opened the door, I ushered him inside. I asked him to take off his shoes and gave him a towel. I showed Ramsey where the bathroom was so he could take off his wet clothes. While he did, I got changed myself.

He wrapped himself in one of my towels while I ran the bath for him. He was still silent. He stayed in the bath for over an hour before he decided to get out. He looked a million times better; his beard was shaved off, he looked clean and he smelled good too. I had to throw his clothes out. They were awful. I managed to find an old pair of shorts that he'd left at my place prior to his disappearance, so I gave those to him to wear.

He laughed as he recognised them and thanked me. Judging from the condition that I found him in, it was obvious he had not eaten for several days, so I had prepared something for us to eat while he was soaking.

"Come Ramsey, I am hungry will you join me for dinner?" He looked at the food and silently approached the table in his shorts. As we ate, we talked. We talked about normal things. That day's events were not mentioned and his disappearance was not one of our conversation topics either. The conversation was kept general. He ate and ate. He tried to do so courteously and with dignity, but I could see he was ravenous.

After dinner he thanked me, graciously. He asked for his clothes and I had to tell him I'd thrown them out. I told him I would get him some tomorrow; he could sleep on the sofa bed. While I made the bed up for him, he asked me: "why are you doing this? I have nothing to give you."

"That's okay Ramsey, I am just happy you're here, safe and well." He got up and hugged me tightly.

"Thank you again."

He held my hand while he spoke.

"It's so hard and lonely out there. It's a tough world on the streets. Very few will turn and look at you when you have nothing. But when you're a somebody the world wants to follow you and be by your side. Help me become a somebody again; I can't do this on my own."

"I will," I promised him. And then I left him to sleep.

The next day, after work, I went on a shopping spree to pick up some things for Ramsey. When I got home, I was surprised to find he had cooked dinner for us both. That was so sweet and thoughtful of him. Roast chicken, vegetables and mash. He loved the clothes I'd bought for him and told me he'd pay me back for them as soon as he could.

After dinner, we sat on the sofa to drink our wine. Ramsey began to open up to me. He had issues; he found it hard to open up to women and feared rejection. He could not find anyone he liked and just found faults wherever he looked. He had never felt ready to commit, he feared getting tangled up in a relationship and getting serious with someone. I wanted to find out more about him and asked whether he mother lived nearby. I hoped she did so that he'd have somewhere to sleep for a few days.

He revealed to me that he grew up with his father. His mother left them when he was nine years old. She'd run off with another man. He'd had more money, a great deal of charm and could give her more than he and his father could. But her new man had given her one condition: she had to leave not only her husband, but her only son, behind.

That had hurt Ramsey deeply. He'd felt the rejection of him and his father very keenly. Ramsey was very good looking with no obvious short comings. But when he told me about his mother, it all became crystal clear. Now I understood him and the problems he had holding on to a woman. The fear he felt about losing her because he would not be good enough. His mother's rejection of him had led him to develop a psychological self-defence mechanism, whereby every woman had a flaw so he needed to move on. He had left behind a string of broken hearted women in his life.

Andrea Aviet

"I am so sorry, I had no clue you experienced all this."
Ramsey explained that he never liked to talk about his history. He needed help but did not know how to go about getting it.

"Don't worry," I told him. "I will get you back on track, we will do it together."

His house had already been repossessed, so that had already been taken care of. His addiction to chat lines was nothing to worry about because Ramsey had no means of getting any money.

"Do you understand Ramsey? It's not real."

"I do", he replied, "I don't know how it got this bad and how I got so deeply involved. I messed up and still owe people money. To get out of one debt I got into another, each time borrowing more in order to sustain myself.

"I couldn't go back to work because I had a bailiff hunting me down. He knew where I worked so I couldn't go back."

5th September – Road to recovery

I knew we needed a plan, so I decided to help Ramsey find a job. He had to start earning again, then he needed support to make sure he did not slip back into his old ways. First, we went to see his GP to get a letter outlining his present mental condition. We could then use the letter to try get his old job back. For help with this, we contacted his union.

We also looked around for support groups to help him with his sex addictions and to help him get back on his feet. He lived with me for a while, and he got his job back. He would hit the gym, cook me dinners every day and life was awesome. He cleaned up really well. I found myself getting physically, mentally, emotionally attracted to Ramsey on every level.

That's when I knew he had to leave. I did not want any complications and was certainly not ready for a relationship. My job with him was done and I was so pleased with the hard work. He'd made some really good progress while living with me, but I did not want to risk something starting up between us. If it failed, Ramsey could easily have slipped back into old ways again.

Well destiny and faith are so complicated.

After dinner, Ramsey turned to me in the kitchen while we were putting the dishes away.

"Thank you for everything, it means a lot to me. You stepped in just as everyone gave up on me and stepped out of my life. Every door closed in my face when I begged for help. Every friend failed to recognise me at that moment, except you."

He stepped towards me. Many times in recent weeks, Ramsey would walk up to me, look into my eyes, and walk away.

I thought he was going to do the same now, but this time it was different. This time, he bent down and kissed me. It frightened me because I was trying my best not to fall in love with him.

"I have wanted to kiss you a thousand times over, but I knew I was not worthy. First, I had to sort myself out before I could hold you in my arms and kiss you. If you don't feel the same way it's alright, you have given me a second chance at life and it's for you that I am going to make it work."

I was so happy to hear those words. His life was given back to him, he'd job reclaimed and he was making really good progress. Pride swelled inside of me. I enjoyed his gentle kiss. Ramsey knew that I was not ready for a man who couldn't everything held together. He knew I needed a man who worked, knew exactly what he wanted and could handle life in any situation that life threw at him.

He understood that I needed someone on whom I could rely. He knew I would support and expect equal support in return. He knew I believed that a relationship is a two-way street of giving and receiving. He had polished up well and was starting to shine. He reminded me of rust being lifted from an old coin; first you see the rust fading slowly, and then it all dissolves. The same old coin, with time, undergoes change and cleans up to look sparkling new and radiant. Yet I did not want to lose the friendship. I told him so.

"I am willing to take any part of you that you're willing to give." As he said those words he came forward and kissed me tenderly again. This time he put some passion into it and stayed by my side longer while he guided my waist gently so as to draw me nearer. He kept me close in his arms and supported me simultaneously. It's hard to describe the feelings I felt then.

The nervousness, the tremor, the warmth of his breath on my lips and his smile. The way he held me so gently, yet tightly. His long masculine arms wrapped around me, making me feel so safe and protected. I loved the way he felt near me, I loved the way he kissed me. Somehow in his arms I felt safe, protected and at peace. He felt so right. My knees weakened and, right then, my heart's desire was Ramsey.

Trying to fight feelings of falling in love can be quite tough and, while he held me in his arms, I felt something stir in me. He lifted my face up and looked straight into my eyes.

"You are beautiful. I have watched you every day. I've seen you smile and I love the positivity you give off. Your strength of character, the way you care for me and the things you do. My love and respect for you has developed and grown, the attraction magnified, and I just want to be with you. Give us a chance?"

We sealed our love that night; there was no stopping our feelings. We bonded from that moment, in every way possible. While he started in the kitchen, we ended up in the bedroom and he made wild, passionate love to me. This was an all-time new experience. Ramsey propped pillows under my bottom to get a better angle of thrusting as he penetrated deep within. That sent me off into screams of pleasure and ecstasy. It wasn't just a bonding of bodies that we experienced that night, but we bonded on an emotional level too. A far greater experience than just having meaningless sex. When you actually feel for each other, everything is magnified in intensity; it's very different from just being lustful and having sex in the heat of the moment. With every motion your emotions bond and you elevate each other.

"I am falling in love with you," he confessed, as he looked deep into my eyes. Fear stopped me from reciprocating and saying out loud the words he longed to hear. The words which, from within my heart, I too longed to whisper. With his head bent down over mine, our foreheads touching, he said, "even if you don't say it, I know you do".

We lay in bed, enjoying each other and our bonding. I don't know when it happened but I fell off to sleep in the comfort of his arms.

The next morning, I woke to the smell of fish. Ramsey had made me breakfast in bed with a red rose on the side of the tray. The curtains had been drawn back and the sunlight filled the room with all its glory.

"Wake up, my love."

Oh, he was doing all the right things. I was unnerved. But I did not want it to end anytime soon. We ate together and then showered together too. He lathered my body with soap, caressing my curves as he went. He told me they were too much for him to resist. I knew it was true because when I turned around he had an erection. We had more in the bathroom under the shower. It was very erotic having sex early in the morning. After a restful night's sleep he was definitely in the swing of it again, his energy levels replenished.

We couldn't hide our emotions at work and it wasn't long before our workmates started asking if we were dating. They remarked that both of us glowed and just seemed to be smiling a lot more. Ramsey and I continued seeing each other for months. It was the best relationship I had been in for a while and it really seemed to be going great. We had planned to go out to celebrate his birthday and I wanted to surprise him with some sexy lingerie. I went home early to decorate the place and try my new underwear on.

On my way home I felt a little excited and also a little anxious. For some reason I felt that I needed to drop in and see Heather and Zara. I wanted to say a thank you again for helping me to understand Ramsey.

Today was the first day I had decided to do a little dance for him and I thought I'd asks the girls to check out my outfit and give me a few pointers. It's silly really, but I was nervous and wanted to keep our sex life passionate. He always tried to spice things up in the bedroom, now it was my turn.

As I entered Zara spotted me. The room was crowed and Heather, as usual, was being Heather;

enticing and trying to get some fellow to stick notes in her bra.

"Hi Zara," I said. "I need to practice a lap dance, learn how to be exotic and enticing."

Zara smiled.

"You're in love or else you would never go to such an extent."

I laughed and said, "I came to thank you and Heather. The man I saved and helped get back on his feet, well, I've fallen in love with him."

Zara seemed concerned.

"Are you sure he's changed? It takes a long time to get out of these addictions even if one has a partner. Sometimes the fantasy addiction is hard to let go of."

"Well Zara he has changed and it's his birthday today."

Just then Heather shouted "Give it up for the birthday boy!" She showed the audience the bundle of notes she'd just received for a lap dance.

"I would love to meet him," said Zara.

We were in the midst of conversation, and I promised to bring him around soon. I knew I would have to wait until he was really stronger, to handle an environment like this without getting sucked into it. We hugged and as I turned I saw the birthday boy receive a lap dance from Heather. She really was good. He had his face buried in her behind as Heather danced around him. She didn't mind letting her punters touch her, which management would let slide since it pulled in the big spenders. If you paid extra you could touch. Zara told me that this guy was a regular, that he spends loads and Heather was his favourite, he was always touching. We started laughing. But my laughter stopped when she stood up from his lap, his hands still all over her.

I saw the lucky guy's face and shock gripped my soul. Tears streamed down my face.

"Ramsey!"

"This is Ramsey? Oh no..."

Heather turned to look at me, shocked. Ramsey saw me then.

"Oh no, baby, wait. Let me explain."

Heather repeated, "Baby? Oh no... I am so sorry, I had no idea. I thought he was just another paying customer."

I felt sick in the pit of my stomach; I dropped the outfit on the floor and walked out as fast as my legs would let me. Ramsey came running after me.

"You were not supposed to see that. I am sorry, I am so sorry I hurt you."

I turned to him, hurt flashing in my eyes.

"So, if I did not see, you would keep on coming here right? How could you? Everything you said and did was a lie. We are over. Take your things and leave. I don't want to hear another word from you, not now, not ever."

I walked out of the building, but Ramsey followed me. He insisted that I owed it to us, to our relationship, to listen to what he had to say. But I'd had enough. There was nothing left to say... Nothing could change the betrayal I felt inside. I had fallen in love with him. He had lived with me, under the same roof and we went to the same work place. He'd told me he was saving for a house so he could get his independence back. So he could be a man that I could love.

What was that? I repeated it all back to him. Was all that just an act? He had betrayed me, he had betrayed us. And he had destroyed true love, which could have turned into something deep and meaningful. He had destroyed my trust and faith. My love for him could not survive this; above all he cheated on me with lies and deception. A lie that he was better, a lie of wanting a normal life with me so that we could build a future together.

I told him, if he had wanted sex that badly he could have told me. I would have paid for him to get someone. Even that would have been better than what he did to me. Ramsey begged. He fell to his knees, on the road, amid all the evening traffic. He didn't care who saw him.

"I love you. I have dreams of marrying you and I was going to propose during dinner. Please, don't walk out of my life," he shouted after me.

I could not believe my ears. I couldn't help myself turning back to him. I slapped him hard across the face and flung the diamond ring he had produced, out of his hands.

"I don't give a fuck! You betrayed me and you have taken everything from me. You're sick, go get help. I hate that I ever let you in, I hate that I fel in love with you."

I walked off then, leaving him kneeling in the street. Ramsey ran after me, but it was no use.

"You're in love with me?"

"No, I thought I was. The one thing I know is that I hate myself right now. I should have let the boys hit you that night. I should have walked away and never come to help you. Get out, get out, get out!"

I broke down uncontrollably then.

"Why, why? I fell in love with you; why you did this to me, to us? Tell me why?"

Ramsey looked at me; he tried to reach for me but stopped,

"Don't you dare touch me with your filthy hands, don't you dare."

Ramsey turned to face a shop window. He rammed his fist through it. The glass shattered and his hands bled.

"I am so sorry, I love you. I really do. But I have a problem. I tried to change. I am nothing without you." He cried on bended knees.

He broke me that day. He killed me. Inside the pain was so excruciating I did not know what to do. I didn't know who to turn to, I could not breathe, I could not sleep, I could not eat. I broke down in tears all day and all night. No one at work ever saw me again. I lost loads of weight. Hours turned to days, days turned to weeks, weeks turned to months. There was no difference between night and day, no difference between life and death. I was dead, he had stripped away my will to live, he stripped away the love I had inside. He took it all, the day he took my trust. He left me for dead. "Why?" The only question I could muster. "Why?" Was I not good enough? What was wrong with me? What did I lack? I should not have fallen for him.

Maybe if we had just had sex, but I hadn't made meaningful love to him. Then it would not hurt this much. Ramsey came every day and banged on my door, Zara and Heather too. I could not care less.

I woke up one day to find myself in hospital on a drip. They said I was dehydrated and looked terrible, like a skeleton. Ramsey, Zara and Heather were in the room with me. A tear ran down my cheek. Zara just stared at me.

"No, no, no my sweet friend, no. Not you, not you."

Ramsey didn't understand why Zara cried.

"What is it? What's wrong? It's good news, she's out of the coma. She's back with us," he said.

Zara looked at Ramsey and put her hand on the side of his cheek.

"No Ramsey, I have seen that look before on many a broken woman. She is not the Rose we knew. This is a very different Rose. One who is lost forever."

Ramsey pushed Zara aside and came to by beside.

"I am so glad you're awake. I have waited for you for a year, I love you more than ever."

I am Rose. It took me three months to recover from my coma and get back on my feet. The day I came out of hospital I decided to let bygones be bygones. I needed money and Ramsey still had his job.

It's ironic how life can turn out to be such a bitch to you. I didn't feel ready to work again, so I decided to be free and do as I pleased.

This led to a new phase in my life.

I went to a bar one night to get some food. At the bar there sat a good looking, well-built man. He was tall and blond. He had broad shoulders. He was handsome. I still hadn't regained all the weight I'd lost so I was extra slim, dressed to kill and had managed to put a full face of make up on before I left the house. I flashed my eye lashes at him and, before long, he appeared next to me, holding his glass of wine. He asked many questions about me, showing lots of interest. We had dinner together and as he walked me to my front door, he kissed me goodnight.

I saw Ramsey coming towards us, across the road.

"Would you like to come in?" I asked the stranger. Ramsey saw him enter.

"No! Please don't." I shut the door.

I changed that night. That was the first night I slept with a complete stranger. I wasn't drunk. I had complete hold of my senses.

As we fucked, I could see flashes of Ramsey on the stage with his head buried in Heather's breasts. Tears rolled down my cheeks.

"Are you okay?"

"Yes, everything's great, thank you."

He continued until he came. Of course, I participated. The next morning, as he stepped out of my house, Ramsey lay asleep on the steps outside. He woke up when he heard my front door close behind me. He got to his feet and punched the stranger on the face.

"Who is he? What's his name?" He shouted, clearly upset.

"I don't know."

"What? You slept with this guy and you don't know his name? Don't you care? What's wrong with you? This is not you, Rose."

Zara appeared at the foot of my steps. Ramsey ran to her, begging for her help.

"What's going on? She's your friend, help me save her, please."

Zara looked at me; she looked into my eyes and said, "I can't Ramsey. Rose is in a place where, even if she wants to, she can't get out."

Andrea Aviet

6th September – Broken

"Walk with me," Zara said to Ramsey, gently.

She explained to him that we had bonded; our souls were interlocked when we slept together. The love bond, the unity, he laid an imprint on me, on my soul.

"The hurt and tragedy Rose feels is because she fell deeply in love with you. The betrayal haunts her; she can't get past it and is on a path to self-destruction, self-ruin. It hurts so much, she can't cope with it."

Ramsey replied, "All that time she was in hospital I never touched another woman, I just could not. It's been a year."

It often happens that, when a person feels extreme emotions, they can snap out of a problematic trait or behavioural pattern. Ramsey's sickness left him when he thought he was going to lose me.

Sadly, it was the love I felt for him which caused me to lose myself. What a sacrifice. How bitter destiny can be. The very life I had set out to save him from, consumed me, taking my life in the same direction.

"I love her with all my heart; I am going to get her back. I don't care how long it takes and no matter how my heart breaks. She is the only woman for me. I got her into this; I am going to get her out."

Weeks, months, years passed. Ramsey never touched another woman, and he waited patiently for me. I slept with any man I came across as long as he paid the bill.

Andrea Aviet

15th October – Transformation

One day I met a lady. She asked me to accompany her to church. She had trouble walking and needed someone to support her. Her walking stick had broken. I declined but went and bought her a new walking stick. The little old lady said,

"Can you walk with me please," she said to me. "I am afraid I am going to fall if I am left on my own."

I helped her to the door, and the pastor came and greeted her. He thanked me dearly for my assistance and invited me in. I was about to say no when the feeble old lady said "Just for a while, just until the music plays?"

"Alright," I said. "Just until the music plays."

I loved music; it was one of the hidden traits which still had some residue left behind within me. When the music stopped I got up and left.

Every week it turned into a sort of habit, whereby I would walk into church with the little old lady, stay during the hymns and then leave.

One day, the little old lady did not feel too well; she started to have breathing problems so I ended up staying for the entire mass. This started to happen on a regular basis. I was still sleeping around. The preacher must have found out about it because, one day, he came down and prayed over me.

"The Father up above does not care what you do. He said to tell you, He sees you for who you are and loves you dearly."

I said nothing; I was quiet. But the need to sleep with another man disappeared from that day onwards.

Was it a sense of understanding right from wrong? Was it a sense of guilt? I don't know, but something changed.

Ramsey paid me a visit shortly after that.

"How are you doing?"

"I am good."

He stood by my side, silently.

"Would you like to go for a coffee?" I asked him.

It had been three long years of torture between the two of us. I never could bear to be near him for more than a few seconds. Yet this time was different. I asked him for coffee. He was over the moon. The man had changed his life around completely. For three years he stayed away from every other woman.

Andrea Aviet

"How are you keeping Rose?" he asked me.

"Well, I am good and you don't need to worry about me anymore," I replied.

"I had to tell you, I have changed. It's been three years and I have not been near a woman."

I was not moved. In fact, I asked him to move out of the neighbourhood.

He looked at me, confused.

"I am going to be by your side until you need me. And even if you don't, I am still going to wait for you, until the last day of my life."

The saddest part was that Ramsey had said something along similar lines to her, before that horrific, traumatic day.

"There will never be an us; you are wasting your time."

A few months past and I got very ill. My depression and anxiety returned. My will to live ceased to exist, I was just an empty vessel. I had to fight my own conflicting demands and struggled to cope with life. I could not hold my own. The past had made me so bitter, angry, sad and unforgiving. It stole the kindness from my soul leaving me crushed. I was on the path to self-destruction and I could see no point in living. I was starving myself; I did not want to eat or drink, and as a result I was taken to hospital again. Now my body had become very weak and unable to fight any sickness.

Ramsey broke down on bended knees and sobbed in the same church that I had started going to.

"Why? Why? Not now, please I beg you. I did wrong, I have waited for three years, don't take her now, take me instead. I love her with all my heart."

The pastor tried to console him. Every day he came and prayed, though he never knew how. He cried out with his feelings and said, "Save the one I love please, I beg you, make her whole again". The greatest love of all, self-sacrifice.

Months passed. Soon it had been an entire year, gone by again. I went through a series of sessions of therapy, counselling; there were no further signs of acute depression and anxiety. It seemed to have worked. Ramsey visited me after my final diagnosis. He lifted me up with joy. He was so happy. I had lost all my beautiful hair. In my upset state of mind I had taken a pair of scissors and cut away all long, beautiful curls. I felt embarrassed to walk out of hospital after being discharged. The hospital let me go, no longer was I self-harming. Ramsey gave me a white satin scarf to wear around my head.

Andrea Aviet

"This will look so beautiful on you."

16th October – Forgiveness mends the soul

As he turned to me and tied the scarf around my head, I looked into his eyes and said, "I forgive you". Ramsey looked at me. He could see life in my eyes once more and, although I had aged, lost my hair, the love was still there. He saw the twinkle and spark come back. There was emotion, there were feelings, he kissed his Rose again and held me in his arms like the first day we had made love. He fell to his knees and sobbed, gently.

"He heard my prayers. He made you whole again. I love you, I love you, I love you!" he cried. "With all my heart and soul I prayed for you to be whole again."

For the first time in four years, I hugged him back.

"I have carried this with me day and night, waiting until the time was right. I have up held the vows without actually proclaiming them out loud in front of man and coronation. In sickness and health, till death do us apart. I have watched you be with others, for the pain I caused you. I have cried every night for a chance at redemption and for a chance to be by your side. To care, to nurture, to love, to support you and to be the man who you fell in love with at first sight.

"Forgive me and make me the proudest man alive by saying yes to being my wife. For without you, there is no life worth living."

I looked at the ring that he had produced and said, teary eyed, "I have nothing to offer you. I slept around so much my body has passed from one man to another. I still could not get rid of the hurt inside until one day, I know not when, God's hand passed over all and made the hurt alright."

He asked again, "Do you love me?"

"With all my heart, till death do us apart."

He screamed with joy. Zara and Heather came running to hug us. It had been a long wait, the sacrifice of love ignited, love lost and love regained. Our story was one of true love, endurance and victory. We had the most magnificent wedding, because of the nature and intensity of true love between us.

For our honeymoon we decided to go to the coast. First, we were to meet up with common friends who were going to travel up with us to Las Vegas. We were as happy as two people could be, new found lovers, the world was ours for the taking. Romance was in the air, true love had stood the test of time.

18th October – Honeymoon

Nick and Sandra came to meet us and drive us down to the Holiday Inn. I watched them, but somehow something did not seem quite right. It was strange to describe and understand. Their relationship seemed different from ours. Well I guess, I have learnt. My quest for understanding people and their love lives, emotions and differences, persisted. On some level I wanted to understand why couples lacked that love, why did the love fizzle out?

Nick just wanted to get married and start a new life. Sandra wanted to get out of her parents' house. They were too strict and never gave her the freedom to do anything she fancied, leaving her trapped and unhappy. The two met at a pub during a birthday celebration of a mutual friend. The conversation flowed and they embarked upon a journey of discovering each other. From being total strangers, interest was ignited, an attraction formed yet they were not in love with each other. The similarities they had were very practical and they each wanted something that only the other could provide. It was like a contract marriage with mutual benefits but no monetary gain.

Sandra needed to leave home so she could do as she pleased and be free. Nick wanted to get married and have a family, since he thought it was time now for him to settle down. He was getting on in age. The once smooth skin on his face now started to wrinkle with fine lines. It's strange, the reasons why couples decide to settle down. Some for love, others for mutual benefits, companionship, monetary gains, longing for children and to leave an heir behind. Whereas others just do it to show that they fit right into society. If you look at the various reasons that cause an individual to pick a certain partner its quite intriguing. Some pick for lust, love, certain length of duration, character etc.

It is quite safe to say, I guess, some for a reason and some for a season. Human nature is so complex. However, once we find a true better, other half, life takes off in an entirely new direction and turns into a higher, more beautiful purpose, where souls engage and love manifests. This is when true human nature can develop into something spectacular whereby life is created or destiny fulfilled. Yet if the wrong partner is chosen, life can be an exceptionally hard; a rocky path to climb up from a life of disaster, pain and suffering.

I see some couple just existing together. Life, being so precious and without a certain set amount of time, should be lived to the fullest with happiness, joy and contentment. Who knows what the future holds? For it is true, although we try to make our own destiny, we are all in the hands of fate, we are all but mere puppets. Our strings are pulled and we live our lives on uncertain, shaky ground. When life will end we know not, nor can any prediction be made.

With all these thoughts going through my mind, I felt it was better to first approach Nick and ask what's going on? However, I did not want to say anything about how wonderful my life had turned out to be. Sometimes people just don't understand the difference between true love and just being together. Often love is confused in terms of staying with each other for long periods of time. There is such a difference between just living together, mere existence or routine and truly wanting to wake up every morning to do something special for the one you love.

True love is the compromise, togetherness and willingness to go beyond your own needs and desires, just to make your partner truly happy.

As I suspected he was more forthcoming than his partner and blurted out "Our relationship is unique".

"I told her I am not in love with her; I have feelings for, and like her, but that's about it. In the long run, love might develop. Who knows, but for now all I want is a family life."

All Sandra cared for was going out, having a good time with her friends, going to the pub, drinking, hanging around with others of her own age. They had formed, between them, a good deal, a mutual agreement. This suited them perfectly but what would happen years down the line? What of the examples they were setting for their children and generations to come? As I always say, all five fingers are not the same, thus each one will have their own unique characteristics, likes, dislikes etc.

Their relationship worked for them although it was not an ideal relationship. But these days you have to classify a relationship as ideal if it fits your lifestyle and requirements. What's good for one is not necessary good for another. We all look and find our happiness in different ways and places. People have different routes but the goal is always the same, in the pursuit of happiness.

Throughout the week Nick would work very hard and do as he pleased, but during the weekend he turned into the best dad and partner. He would look after the kids, cook dinner, teach and bathe them while Sandra hit the bars with some of her female friends, drank, partied and had fun all night long.

Was this an appropriate way for a lady to behave? Not really, but we have to look deeper into the 'why' she did something, the causes etc. Going back into Sandra's past, she felt that her life had been stolen from her. When she was young, clubbing, drinking, dancing, having a good time with friends was something she longed for. When you are deprived of something growing up and then suddenly find out you yourself are a mum, how do you cope? How do you handle all the responsibility? Do you feel robbed? Do you begrudge you circumstances?

I have learnt the answer is self-love, understanding, finding yourself and taking responsibility for children at the same time. These children were given no choice. They were brought into the world because you created and conceived them.

The best way to describe the character conflict within Sandra was discovered while finding herself; Sandra had been deprived, held back self. She had been bound with heavy chains which hung from head to toe. Chains of bondage, chains of ownership and belonging. Sandra's parents thought they were doing the best for her, but they stole her childhood, they stole experiences of mischief and fun. She was deprived of making history, memories, learning from follies and becoming a sharp, responsible person.

Time has taught me well to understand, that which has gone, will not return. We need to have the realisation that we can gain what we deserve out of life while there is still time. We can't return to our childhood, yet we can excel into professionalism and gain more than we lost. Reinvention for progression rather than regression is the concept we must adopt.

How we choose to reinvent ourself is most important. That is exactly what I learned from Sandra. Although she felt she had missed out on a childhood of discovery, she coped by choosing a partner who suited her needs. The relationship worked for them. Both got what they needed and the children seemed to be doing great.

What works for you? So many of us are caught up in an idealist ideology where we expect things to come packed in this particular way, so it looks great and appropriate to all who see it.

The next important question is how does it feel to you, when no one is around, when it's not packaged but uncovered in its naked form? When it's just you and your partner, behind closed doors, how does the relationship feel?

Think about these questions. They are useful questions to ask and the only one who matters is you. *You* need the answers. On my journey, I've learned about so many different relationships, so many different people, different situations. Each so unique in their own way.

20th October – Sin City

After we spent some time on the coast, we headed up to Las Vegas, 'Sin city'. I'd already written a list of places and attractions I wanted to see.

First on my list was the Fremont Street Experience, better known as Glitter Gulch, located on a five-block section under a 90-foot-high canopy. There were lights, sound and music playing all the time. Before the show, all businesses turned off their lights as a signal that the show was about to start. Meanwhile, on the Strip, The Mirage boasted a volcano which would erupt to a soundtrack of actual volcanic eruptions. This would happen every night after 8pm. There was the Secret Garden and the Dolphin Habitat; a large aquarium with 450 different species of fish. Caesar's Palace and The Colosseum. These were just a few among the many I had planned to visit first.

The guys were discussing going to strip clubs such as the Trenzs. The law in Vegas is such that clubs can only have either alcohol *or* nudity. They cannot provide both. That, I was told, explained why most of the bars merely advertised topless shows, so they could still serve alcohol. The Palomino Club is the only club to provide full nudity.

At more than 40,000sqft, Crazy Horse III had plenty of stages spread out over several rooms. Located just west of Mandalay Bay, it was one of the more accessible strip clubs from the south end of the Strip. It was very clean and felt like a nightclub. Cover could be as high as $50 but you'd never be charged if you called the free limo service to pick you up. (So, order the free limo! The club even had a smartphone app for it.) The main room had a 50ft-long bar (to make it easy to order a drink) and elevated seating (to make it easy to watch the girls). Open 24 hours a day, seven days a week, with a late-night food menu and some surprisingly tasty sushi, CH3 was also a great spot to watch a big game or UFC fight, with HDTVs scattered around the venue. But maybe you should be paying attention to the stage anyway.

One of the largest strip clubs in Vegas, Sapphire had more than 70,000sqft of poles, stages, and private Champagne-filled skyboxes to check out the hundreds of girls who performed on any given night. The place actually used to be a fitness club before it was renovated into a palace of skin and silicone. There was even a pool out back for daytime club-style partying during the warm summer months. Rent a cabana or daybed and check out the 'aquarium' filled with beautiful women treading water. However, our favourite indoor feature was the 'Rockstar Lounge' with a glass-top view of the girls dancing above. Packages came with a free limo ride and cover included. For the ladies, there was a male revue known as the

'Men of Sapphire' that played in a separate room on Thursdays, Fridays, and Saturdays.

I had no interest as I had my share of strippers when trying to save my beloved.

But the choice they offered was endless; from single men, to women and even activities for partners. The city never sleeps and it's amazing to see.

Well Ramsey and the others were still up for checking out the strip joint. It was just a matter of deciding which one to go to.

The city of lights, glamour, action, excitement and two sides. One is wild with passion, excitement the other all professionalism. It's there we met Max. Let me describe Max. He was tall and tanned. A perfect figure of excellence and temptation beyond human comprehension and belief. I stripped him naked in my imagination. Never had I seen such beauty, good looks ever before. Ted knew instantly that I was mentally sinning.

"You're getting attracted, aren't you?"

"Oh yes, I am, I don't mean to but I am getting attracted."

Ramsey smiled and remarked he could read me like a book. He was not cross, nor was he upset. We are human beings. I was in love with him, yet the sexual, uncontrollable urge just to be fucked by Max was becoming a desire which my body started longing for. Little did I know Max was a gay prostitute and stripper.

While I desired Max, he in turn was eyeing up Ramsey. Talk about triangular attraction. Well Ramsey had a mischievous sense of humour. He said, well we are in Vegas so we are going to have fun my way. He proposed we went to a strip joint.

"Is that alright with you honey? Are you up for that?"

"Fine, let's go."

Being open to experimenting, excitement and exploring, I was up for anything that night. Sex excited me; show me one person with any sexual preference who doesn't get excited by the thought of sex?

We entered a room in a strip club, all excited. Sandra was a little crazy just like me. As we got in she started eyeing up the men.

"Which one do you like? I like him!" she exclaimed. "Oh, I want to see him butt naked, over your right shoulder."

He was cute. All of a sudden, I realised there were too many men and no women.

"Where are the other women?" I asked Ramsey. "There seems to be more men than women in here."

He did not answer. He just smiled, took me by the hand and said: "Observe closely, my gorgeous." With the start of the music, my excitement rose to an all new height.

It was Max. He was on stage and he was dancing, stripping. I tell you, he had skill which blew my biological system into acceleration mode. Desires of lust overtook me. I craved his touch, I could imagine him close to my naked body. His sweat poured down his six packs. The energy he had was amazing, I could visualise us in bed together as being a fantastic pair. Ramsey was observing me closely. My eyes twinkled, my moistened lips desired him and my body craved him inside me. All that it was mounting up to was one moment of steamy sex and then it would be fine. I am sure desires would calm down after.

There were no deep-rooted feelings ignited besides lust. Within a few moments the spark from my eyes turned to disappointment and within the pits of my stomach I felt so sick that I vomited. Max was gay. He preferred Ramsey, and every other man, compared to me. Oh my God, I rushed out leaving the rest there. Ramsey came running after me.

Andrea Aviet

"Are you alright?" I vomited. Ramsey called a taxi and took me to the hotel to get some rest.

While I lay in bed, I felt rotten, guilty, confused and disbelieving. He came and kissed me.

"I am so sorry, I have to apologise. The attraction I felt towards Max was so great that I literally imaged us being together, forgive me."

He smiled, "I know you did, our love is stronger. Even if you walked into a room alone with Max and he made advances on you, you would find the strength to walk away."

Then I slept.

Ramsey came to check up on me.

"Are you feeling better darling?" He put his hand at the side of my face gently as he asked.

"Yes, much better." Ramsey leaned in to kiss me. "Well, Max is not here. Would you mind if I fill in?"

He had a mischievous way about him and such sense of humour. "I aim to please and have a reputation of never disappointing."

Well the next thing I knew, Ramsey was stripping and dancing to music; yes, he was doing a striptease for me. Since he too was in fantastic shape there was no doubt in my mind he could and would make it big in the strip joint if ever he wanted to try out.

He worked hard Finally, he undressed me. It led to a very romantic, exciting love making session where, although I never thought it would be possible, he managed to elevate both of us. He was amazing and it just felt so different this time. It felt perfect.

Andrea Aviet

22th October – I love you

Lying in bed together he said, "I love you with all my heart but I just wanted to teach you the very lesson you taught me. Don't fall for appearances. That which is packaged so beautifully may not be exactly what you desire."

I smiled "I love you too Ramsey, I really do."

I leaned up on my elbow and looked him in the eye. "Forgive me, for I was sinning against us. It was one moment of weakness."

"We are only human," he replied. "It's easy to fall into meaningless temptation and in turn ruin true love. I am glad, though, we had an amazing time; each time I make love to you it's like being with you for the very first time."

Then with a kiss he went off. I could hear him singing and the pots and pans in the kitchen were being tossed about. He was getting breakfast ready. He was amazing.

We got ready after breakfast and went shopping. This was the best vacation we had ever experienced. It was amazing. The lights, the energy, the people, the atmosphere. Everything all together was just a brilliant combination. As I was walking down the street with him we were noticing all these different couples. It was intriguing to see. The variance between ages, professions, ethnicity and religion. But there seemed to be a common goal of 'enjoyment' binding them all together.

One couple stood out. They caught Ramsey's attention, oddly enough. Las Vegas is Las Vegas so you expect anything to happen. Nothing is unexpected for Sin City. However, although I'm an open-minded, liberal thinker this couple in particular caught my attention. Sandy and Luke were a fantastic couple. Luke was in his late 40s and Sandy was more towards her early 40s. They were a good match. I watched the way Sandy looked at Luke. The gentle way she laid her hands on his. She looked so pleased while they shopped together and enjoyed taking his advice. He, in turn, enjoyed choosing compatible fabrics, cosmetics, jewellery, shoes. They had a bond whereby, they could truly, deeply, enjoy all womanly activities together.

Sandy never had to compromise. We learned a great deal about them because we got talking to them over coffee and offered to take them for dinner just so that we could have a chat. Let me back track. I had entered a shop looking for jewellery but I remained there for over an hour and could not make up my mind as to which piece of jewellery I preferred. That's when Sandy and Luke entered. Luke was absolutely amazing. He spoke about colour combinations, clarity, the cut, which one he felt matched my features better and would help me stand out in a room full of people. He was better than the shopkeeper.

During dinner, we actually realised that Luke was in fact 'Lacy'. Let me explain. Sandy kept referring to Luke as Lacy. In the very beginning we thought Sandy and Lacy were lesbian lovers. It was only later, at dinner, when Lacy went into the gents' toilet and came out as Luke. We were stunned, speechless. Yes, you got it. Luke was transgender.

I wondered how they had come to be together? Had they got together as Sandy and Luke and Luke had later become Lacy? How did she cope with this intriguing behaviour? It was not easy to understand. How can you be with a man who desires to be a man at one moment and a lady at the next?

All I can say is Sandy was unique and special. There is no other way to describe her. Compelling curiosity took hold of me. There was a story between the two of them and I felt the need to uncover it.

The burning question which baffled me was why did she stay?

My line of questioning had to be delicate, polite and respectful to their individual needs. I had to make sure no boundaries were crossed and that my line of questioning did not offend.

So, I started, subtly, by trying to break the ice.

"Where did you two meet?"

They met at a music fair, they told me.

"How long have you been together?"

"Four years this summer," replied Luke.

"It's been quite a journey," Sandy remarked.

"How do you mean?"

"Well our relationship is quite different from others. It's unique. We met at a music convention, started to date, but all along Luke had confided in my that he was not comfortable. Before we could take our relationship any further, he wanted to show me something. At first, I thought, maybe he had a child with an ex-partner. Then insecurity started to torment me, as I really liked him. I thought to myself 'is there a crazy ex?' 'What is it that is so upsetting for him?' 'What is it that frightens him?'"

Luke had told Sandy, though he was falling in love with her, there was only one thing which could keep them apart, and that was her alone. Confusion, took hold of Sandy. She started to feel that maybe, just maybe, he was playing games with her and was not genuine. She was to meet Luke for dinner in their favourite restaurant where he was to reveal to her the deepest secret which would probably be the end of them, he warned her.

An anxious Sandy waited patiently for Luke to appear. As soon as the clock struck 7pm, a lady walked up to Sandy.

"May I sit with you?"

Her hair was in perfect, neat curls. She wore a gorgeous pink dress paired with beautiful white stilettos shoes, a white leather handbag and baby pink lipstick. Her makeup was flawless. It looked professionally done and even better than Sandy's, she thought. As she looked at her, the woman had a strikingly familiar resemblance to Luke!

She smiled at Sandy.

"Are you alright Sandy?"

The woman took a seat next to me. Sandy was speechless. Firstly, she knew her name, next she resembled Luke. No, no wait a minute. Was she Luke?

"Is that you, Luke?" she asked. She had no idea how to react, what to expect to hear.

"Yes, it's me Sandy," Luke replied.

Sandy needed time. Luke was the man she was in love with. She have never bonded so well with anyone ever before. But could she accept this? If yes how was she supposed to cope with it? If not, Luke had said it would be the end of them. Luke stretched his hand out and lay it upon Sandy's. As he did he said, "I love you, but I needed you to see me, I need you to see all of me and love me completely, not partially.

"It's a big ask, but can you? Take your time, as long as you need. It has taken me all my life..."

Sandy was still silent, in shock; passers-by stared as Luke held her hand. From afar it must have looked like lesbian love but only she knew close up, up front it was harder; it was Sandy being in love with a transgender person. He finished dinner. He'd told her he wanted to be known as 'Lucy'. So Lucy walked Sandy home and wished her a goodnight. There were no romantic, long kisses with tongues rolling, just a respectful goodnight.

As Sandy reached her apartment on the ninth floor, she had to do a soul search. It was not easy; she took out a sheet of paper and wrote Lucy on one half. The other, had Luke written on it.

She wrote everything down what she loved about Luke. Lucy had a few qualities she liked which resonated well with her female side.

Andrea Aviet

Wait a minute, she thought to herself, of course they will be the same, they are the same. A person does not change completely; it's just a different side to them. A craving desire to temporarily be something else. Could she accept all Luke's, sides. Could she accept Lucy?

Well she had to re-evaluate clearly. Luke was the best thing which had happened to Sandy in a long while. He was the man she wanted to spend her life with. They would definitely be one of those couples who could grow old together and make their own memories, history. He was understanding, kind and supportive. Yet, Lucy was in the picture, how would she deal with her? After assessing the situation and coming to the conclusion that under no circumstances could she afford to lose Luke, Sandy could see that the only way forward was to accept Lucy too. While Luke remained her partner and lover, Lucy became her friend. In time, after a lot of adjustment, she had found a lover where the benefit of both worlds lay in her hands.

A friend to shop with and man to make love to. What more could she ask for? Luke was shocked when she told him that she loved him for him. None of us is perfect. Sandy would be foolish to let go of the one thing in her life I was absolutely sure of. He could not believe his ears, she recalled, he sobbed and said, "if only you knew how terrified I was to reveal the secret I held within, just because I feared,

I would have to let you go." As he said this, they just kissed.

Oh, I was already teary eyed but what Ramsey and I were not expecting was that Luke had decided to ask Sandy to marry him. Today, on this very day, their anniversary and walking down memory lane.

The narration was beautiful and the proposal, splendid. It was like in the movies; he got down in the centre of the street on bended knees and asked her," Will you marry me?"

It began to rain all of a sudden and the two just stood laughing, kissing in the rain. They explained to us, on the day they got together it rained; it was symbolic to them, as if the angels were blessing them from above. How beautiful it is to see true love in all its glory. We speak of unconditional love, sacrifice and eternity. What about unconditional acceptance even when it goes against our very own beliefs? What then?

Sandy and Luke taught me, love does not come polished and perfect as we envision it to be. We have to accept the positives, iron out and deal with the negatives, but retain the bond of love so we grow and develop. Love comes in its raw form. You must smooth the rough edges out and make it perfect.

Andrea Aviet

1st Nov – Drag Queen

Well we walked away trying to find shelter from the rain, and strangely enough, walked straight into a gig. There danced this slim beautiful figure of a lady. She had a big hair do, sparkling clothes with stones sown in, stilettos; she was gorgeous. She had high cheek bones, a slender face, eyes as blue as the sea and pink cheeks. She was most delicate looking and when she took a break for a rest, it left me speechless. The gorgeous lady, when she spoke, sounded just like a man...

Really, could it be? Was she a he? Not a chance, I thought to myself. But when I got closer, I realised she had an Adam's apple. She was definitely a he. Oh my God, he was the most beautiful, elegant drag queen.

He put many of us women to shame. He was sincerely breathtaking and very "fishy", Which in drag terms means very feminine. Her name was Nancy. She was funny, spectacular, and encouraged the men to play and touch. She teased her audience and the entire environment felt full of life. Nancy headed off straight to the dressing room after finishing her show and seemed to be there for quite a while. Curiosity was driving me crazy.

A while later, Nathan came up to us, introduced himself, and ordered a beer. Honestly, he had not even a single resemblance to Nancy. Ramsey drew my attention to the fact that Nancy and Nathan were one and the same. He was a normal bloke. He was not attracted to men but liked to dress up for fun.

However, Nathan had other male drag friends who were interested in men... Oohh la la! Being a drag queen meant they could look gorgeous, be a woman, flirt with men, have fun and just let their hair down. It was a fascinating, colourful and glamorous world of beauty.

So, curiosity got the better of me. I wondered how come Nancy did not desire men? Well, Nathan explained, not all drags are gay. Some are straight and prefer to dress as women just for the fun of it. He felt comfortable and at ease, as if a part of him was complete when he turned into Nancy. We all have desires, another side to us. Some might be to be a whore, others a seductive temptress. Whatever inner personality or longing you feel, you should allow yourself to be yourself. I feel life is too short; exploration, and not suppression, leads to satisfaction.

Why suppress yourself? Can you tame a lion? People's personalities when suppressed always manifest into something else negative, and take on a different substitute. That substitute is often harmful, such as alcohol or drugs, since they try to replace it with something less appealing.

It's sort of like loving music but replacing it with dancing. Although the two go hand in hand, if you have two left feet you're not going to enjoy music, no matter how hard you try. That's why I always laugh at people when they try to change themselves to fit in or be perfect in society's eyes. The only perfection one should concern oneself with is self-perfection, inner reflection and acceptance. The rest of the world does not matter. Trying to be something you're not, living a make believe lifestyle leaves you empty, broken, looking into the mirror and wondering who am I?

Personally, I love the fact that Nathan was proud of being himself. He had a level of confidence and comfort to recognise who he wanted to be. Not being afraid of who he was gave him the freedom to explore his sexuality, cravings and desires to the maximum.

In conclusion, Nathan lived a life of no regrets, no what if's, no might bes or possibilities which could have been. He led a life of probabilities and total freedom. There's a lot to learn from individuals displaying self-acceptance and happiness. Often, I find the best way to be is only concerned about yourself. Maybe it sounds selfish, right? But if protecting your inner peace is classified as being a little selfish, then perhaps we all need to be?

We took leave of Nathan as we were extremely tired. Ramsey had expressed a desire to do something exciting before we left Vegas and I knew just what would add that special kinky, unforgettable moment with my man. When we got inside the hotel room Ramsey went to pour out two glasses of wine but looked shattered. We were both exhausted, but it was our last night. It had to be unforgettable. I had kept a secret, away from his prying eyes. Something which would make his exhaustion non-existent, breathe freshness and excited energy into him... I had planned a night which he would never forget. Considering our history and relationship together, this secret of mine would tip the scales to one side – the side of kinky, pure sexual pleasure.

"Are you ready, darling?" I asked.

Without looking, Ramsey replied, "I am baby." I'd dimmed the lights and put some soft music on in the background. As he sat on the leather sofa, shirt off waiting for me and bed, he hadn't even noticed the change in the lighting. The first thing he heard was a whip lash against the floor. Caught unaware, it made him jump and spill some of the red wine down his smooth well defined, muscular chest. As he looked over he saw me dressed to get undressed by my hand alone. He was beyond words.

"What the hell?"

"Shush," I said. "Quiet. You're in my hands now. It's time for you to call me mistress." Ramsey smiled with excitement. He knew my secret was out. I was his very own dominatrix.

He was about to feel the pleasure, the pain, every emotion I wanted him to feel. Punishment at my will, I was in control; he was going to be a victim under my deepest, darkest, fetish desire.

Hell yes, now it was my time to play. No leather boots, no hooks and nails, I was not into that sort of pleasure pain. He watched in utter awe, not knowing what to expect. First my whip slid across his chest, the black handcuffs went on around his wrists and I tugged at them to make sure they were tight. Like a lamb to the slaughter, he sat clueless in anticipation of my every move. The blank blind folds were on and the whip hung around his neck as I led him to the bedroom. I lay him on the bed, face down. I stood on his back with my stilettos the slight pain sent sensations down his body. I turned him over and walked on him again, being very careful not to stand on his hard, erect penis. The imagination is a powerful tool. Although I found it difficult, at first, to inflict pain on him, I soon got into the role play and it took it to an all new level. Getting carried away I lashed him a little harder, harder. We had agreed on a signal if it was getting too much. He had to raise his index finger.

"Are you ok?" I asked.

"Yes mistress." he replied.

"That's good, you're my good boy."

Next, I gagged him, it made me feel empowered. It got me excited as I rotating my metal claw nail around his penis, along the shaft. I twirled my claw around his glands after pulling back the foreskin. He moved his head lifting his chin, his chest swelled with air. I guess he felt a little nervous about how carried away I was getting. I had bought a strap-on but I was still unsure about using it. I held Ramsey's attention. His erection was still going strong. I could tell he wanted me to ride him, and longed to be finished off, he longed to feel me on him. The punishment of not being able to participate was torture for him. I ran my claw down the centre of his chest making a deep red scratch. He moved. It hurt, I could tell, but he never raised his finger. I licked it to sooth his wound. He tried to reach for me but the hand cuffs would not let him. Restriction, desire, temptation, frustration was mounting up. I started to drip, I was wet, and my alter ego was having fun. He felt how wet I was when I sat on his thigh and just then he came. Sperm ran down his shaft and fell at the side of the bed. I laughed; it was a long-held desire of mine to make him come without me actually having sex with him. Men can't resist sex. Temptation and being restrained was driving Ramsey crazy. He deserved a kiss and, as I un-cuffed him and removed the blindfolds, I put the whip down at the side of the bed. He looked at me, grabbed me with both hands and kissed me. Instantly he tore my netted strappy nightdress off, wiped himself clean and said, "Do you realise how much I love you. You never seem to stop amazing me, you're incredible. I love it best when you're wearing nothing at all." He held me tight and would not let go.

He had a sexual appetite which was like mine, unquenchable. That was the secret of our passion. We could have sex morning, noon and night, always willing to try new techniques, keep the excitement going and appreciate each other. From pure, simple love making to role play, submission and empowerment bedroom activities. Yet never did we demean each other. Sometimes dominatrix sex can be taken through different levels from pegging to hurtful, painful pleasure. I guess it depends on individual preference and your partner's desires. While we lay still on the bed and took a rest, he played with me. He stroked the sides of my breasts, ribs, waist and thighs and said he just did not want to let go. I felt love, safety in his arms, comfort and then after a while I felt him become hard while he pressed himself against my buttocks from behind. His fingers reached down and parted my thighs gently.

"Are you ready?"

I looked at him and smiled, he wanted to be inside of me, he pushed in from behind; truly I was frustrated and was longing for his every touch. He started slowly, gently and then started to get vigorous. Having him inside, feeling his hands on my body, felt amazing. After a while of trying different positions that we both enjoyed, our climax came, together. It was mutual; it was fulfilling and left us both content. The best part is experimenting, which brought us closer to each other.

We lay in each other's arms, catching our breath, regaining our energy. In the silence of the night, we both felt the closeness and love between us. We showered together and headed straight to bed; we had a long flight back home the next morning.

I woke up to the smell of fresh coffee and a single rose on my pillow beside me. Ramsey walked over, kissed me and told me it was time to get up. He treated me so well. Where had the time gone? I loved him more than anything. Our journey had not been the easiest, but it had withstood the test of time. We lasted because we truly loved and respected each other and wanted to be together.

We made it to the airport on time. While we sat waiting, I glanced at my other half who just seemed to be staring at me.

"Are you okay?" I asked.

"Yes," he replied with a smile. "I am just trying to understand how you feel. Tell me what you discovered?"

5th November – What do we want?

It seems like such a simple question. But I knew that he meant my quest to record, analyse and uncover the truth between love, lust, fantasy, reality, hidden secrets and alter egos. What makes a relationship last? What makes a man desire only you? Why does he run and when do you become the centre of his entire being?

It's hard to sum up in a few lines. People, irrespective of sexual preference, are still human beings. The colour of our blood, irrespective of gender, race, religion, is still red. We all have one soul and form soul ties with our perfect partner. What defines perfection is our own search for meeting a partner who adequately satisfies our every desire, our being and existence. It's true that no man can live as an island. We all need each other, although we are all flawed with imperfections.

I discovered the only way to be happy and get the partner of your dreams is to know, firstly, who you are. To accept what you are, acknowledge what you desire, don't be afraid of self-realisation. I have learned that confidence is the key to a successful relationship.

Andrea Aviet

A confident partner never fears insecurity, which is the main issue that suffocates a relationship. So many women unknowingly run after a man. They demand his loyalty, time, commitment and this scares him off. Men are born hunters. They like to run free and play the field, as my friends like to point out to me on numerous occasions. Why do females like to commit so soon? Why do they go on a date and dream of potentially getting married, kids, settling down and growing old together? As a woman you might know yourself, know your self-worth. But have you ever questioned, did your partner or date have the time to figure out how valuable you really are? Don't make a man feel that you're too demanding and make him regret his decision. If he is relaxed he will run to you. You will be a joy to be with. Then it's not a necessity or obligation, it's a choice. He chooses you.

Space and time are two factors which go hand in hand. Breathe, enjoy life, take the time to prioritise and put your own needs first. I guarantee your partner will value you more, when you stop trying to do things together too early on in your relationship. When first starting out, let there be space. Take things slow, easy, enjoy the dating process. Take the time to do the things you each like. Don't encroach on each other's boundaries. Show your man you're independent.

Men love their own space, and a woman who can give them freedom along with trust. Be fun-loving and exciting – these are more attractive than the lady who is needy.

When a man has to run after you, work hard to get your interest, the desire to get you is greater.

After all we all appreciate the car or house we had to struggle and save up for. It took hard work, dedication, time, focus and savings.

Which brings me to my next question: what are you giving your partner to focus on? Whether we want to admit it publicly or not, are you painting a picture that you are the one for him or you were just a mistake? A temporary fix to the problem of loneliness?

I realised, throughout my journey of discovery, love is the one common factor that we are all hunting for. True acceptance inspires us. There are countless possibilities of relationships. From same sex, to group living, lesbian relationships, bisexual relationships, gay relationships... call it what you like, but the essence is still the same. The quest to find that one perfect love. The partner who will add joy and meaning to life, and elevate you.

If we all want love so badly, why do so many fail? I figured out quite quickly, domination comes into play. Some want to rule over their partners. Others just get bored in time. I have often heard a woman say that her partner looked so cute when they were first going out, but later he just did not care anymore.

It's important to look good, feel good and realise there are plenty of fish in the sea. There are also plenty of fishermen casting their nets with the hope of landing a good catch. Just because you have someone, does not mean the relationship is set in stone. Never neglect your physical appearance or yourself. A healthy relationship needs to evolve in time; it has to be worked upon, needing nurture. Take the time out of life's busy schedule to make some time for your relationship, friends and hobbies. I stress upon this because all this helps you relax, retain your individual personality. It helps you not just be caught up with each other, but keeps the relationship fresh. Each part of your life has a place; set time aside for each part.

Women, look in the mirror and say: "I am confident. I love myself and I am going to get me a worthy man, who deserves me."

Ramsey laughed when I shared my thoughts with him. He found this line in particular very amusing. Many a truth lies hidden behind this line. Many a time, due to loneliness, people rush and get into relationships which are not necessarily good for them. Why? Because they fear they will miss out.

Some fear their biological clock is ticking and they won't have children. Ask yourself, is it more important to raise a child in a happy environment or is it more important to just have a child?

If you're strong enough to be on your own and raise a child in a stable, happy environment go ahead. If you feel that being with a same sex partner you can still create a loving environment for a child, go ahead. My advice: Never rush. Time is endless, life is accountable.

Confidence leads to positivity. The emphasis is most important, what you feel inside is what you portray outwardly. When I am at home and put cream on my skin, do a hot oil hair therapy, paint my nails, put on sexy underwear, realistically speaking I feel good. Why? Because I pampered myself, I did not wait for anyone else to do it for me.

That's the key ingredient. Don't wait for anyone else to make yourself feel like a million dollars. Time, life, possibilities will pass you by and you will have 'what ifs', questions will be your only companions.

I'll let you in on a secret. Men love confidence in a woman. It's an irresistible attraction. The harder they have to work on getting you, the more appealing you become.

Andrea Aviet

"When are we going to try the strap-on?" Ramsey asked me, after admitting he found my confidence the sexiest part about me.

"Later, when we get home, if you're a good boy."

"I loved it when you took charge and spoke in that tone," he told me. "I could take you right now, put you over my knee, spank you..."

Our message to you: we are all different. Difference is not negative – it's what defines us. Love is what we are all searching for. Where you find it, and with whom, does not matter. The only thing that is important is how your partner treats you and what you feel.

Explore who you are, let your sexuality loose, be free and be yourself.

"Upon a star I wish for love, I wish that true love in all its glory finds you."

By Andrea Aviet

Meet the author

My name is Andrea Aviet. I strongly believe and live by one belief if you "think it" you can "achieve it". "Be free, be happy and take charge of your own destiny, like I have."

My first book was 'White Sorrow a true life story. I am a mother, award winning author, survivor, inspirational fundraiser and global goodwill ambassador. I am always looking forward to supporting causes dealing with the youth, woman and children.

Contact me on:-
Facebook- Andrea Aviet
Website: - www.andreaaviet.com
Email-andreaaviet@gmail.com

Love Andrea xxx

Andrea Aviet